Branches blown down in winter or spring storms littered the street; twice we had to get out to move limbs too large to drive over. Three autumns' worth of unraked leaves decomposed quietly. One of the stained-glass windows in the Methodist church was shattered; an overachieving clump of dandelions grew on the sill.

As we turned onto Main Street, we were both startled to hear a bell clang several times, the last note hanging in the air like an unkept promise.

"What the hell?" was all that BJ said.

Two more blocks and I pointed out the answer. BJ's tiny front yard was neatly trimmed. Clustering around the step was a group of women, fifteen or twenty of them, smiling and waving wildly at us. One of them ran onto the porch, grabbed an iron wand, and struck a rusted iron triangle which hung from a porch rafter on a length of vinyl clothes-line . . .

About the Author

Molleen Zanger lives in the thumb of Michigan with her mate, her son and their friend, as well as three dogs, two cats and a collection of cacti and succulents. She was born in Panama C.Z. and raised mostly in Michigan. Among other things, she has worked as a postal carrier, bartender, real estate sales associate and staff writer/photographer on a weekly newspaper. As she completes her B.A. at Saginaw Valley State University, she accumulates grad school catalogs and sleeps with an atlas near her bed. She frequently traces escape routes from Michigan winters.

THE YEAR SEVEN

BY
MOLLEEN ZANGER

The Naiad Press, Inc.
1993

Printed in the United States of America on acid-free paper
First Edition

Edited by Christine Cassidy
Cover design by Pat Tong and Bonnie Liss
    (Phoenix Graphics)
Typeset by Sandi Stancil

Library of Congress Cataloging-in-Publication Data

Zanger, Molleen, 1948–
    The year seven / by Molleen Zanger.
        p.   cm.
    ISBN 1-56280-034-5 : $9.95
    1. Lesbians—Fiction.   I. Title.
PS3576.A53Y4   1993
813'.54—dc20   92-41009
                                                        CIP

*This book is dedicated
to Kathleen Meyer,
the friend of my heart
and of my soul
and of my mind.*

Acknowledgments

Special thanks go to the Columbia Women Writers (especially Marti, Marge and Val), Dr. Ann Green of Jackson Community College, Sue Messer, and Lua Gutierrez, friends and readers extraordinaire. Thanks also to my kids — Stacy, Scott and Kevin — and to MJ Ogden for unfailing moral support.

CHAPTER 1

I have been sitting here for over an hour, trying to decide where to begin, and how much to tell. Nancy watches me with her cellophane-blue eyes, wondering, no doubt, what I'm doing. But not why. If she ever wondered why anyone did anything, there is no sign of it left.

Curiosity died with the rest of our world. Murdered. We don't know whom to accuse. I wish I could point a righteous finger and say, "Them. They did it! They did it with chemicals, or germs or an energy source they only pretended to comprehend."

Or maybe it was just negligent homicide. Just *oops*.

Hell, maybe it wasn't anyone's fault; maybe extraterrestrials, or a vengeful God, just got overzealous one day. One day in July. July 17. Seven years ago.

Nancy's birthday. Funny, huh? Her twenty-third birthday. I had turned twenty-one the month before. She told me her mother had baked her a cake. Angel food with pink icing drizzled down the sides and nonpareils sprinkled on top. No candles; her mother disapproved of candles. People blowing spit all over cakes. Germs, you know.

Nancy felt nauseated when she got home from Jackson City Hall where she typed the day's quota of marriages, divorces, births and deaths into the statistic-hungry computer. More irony. Almost funny. Just think how overloaded that damn computer would have been the next day.

Nancy had lain on her chenille bedspread and fallen asleep, or passed out, or something.

She told me the nausea was still with her when she woke up, and stayed with her several days. But that could have been caused by finding her parents and little brother dead on the living room floor. Pretzel, her dog, too. Dead. No blood, no gore, nothing. Just quiet. She went outside to call a neighbor and there was more quiet. No cars, no power-line hum. No lawn mowers, no dogs barking or kids screaming. Nobody calling to come in for dinner or turn down that damn TV. She went to the nearest neighbor and found them dead, too. She went from house to house and found them all the same, their occupants dead, as if ritually sacrificed.

So she went home and sat in front of the blank-screened TV, her family at her feet, and waited for her turn, or a special message from the President. A miracle.

That's all she remembers. She doesn't even remember meeting me.

We had all lived so long, it seemed, with the certainty of just such an occurrence — an Armageddon — that it was anticlimactic when it finally happened.

It seemed perfectly natural for everyone to just drop dead. Almost everyone, that is.

The surprise was that there were no high-level explanations or apologies. But of course, there were no more communications systems, no more newspapers or televisions.

"I don't mind dying, I only want to know how I went." No one said that, but someone should have.

I still want explanations, I want answers. Who and what and where and when and why and why and why.

Most of all, I want to know — why not all? Why didn't *I* die? Or Nancy?

Oh, there were others, too. Women, a few, stiff-legged, staring like zombies. I left the city as much to escape them as the stench of 35,000 rotting corpses, not counting animals.

One of the zombie-like women stiff-legged up to me. She was gray. All gray. Hair and shining eyes and skin. She wore a large, gray, man's cardigan. It looked like a dress on her. She plucked at my sleeve, over and over like a guitar string, and said, "What. What. What. What."

All in the same tone of voice, flat and monotonous, gray. But she didn't really seem to see me. It was as if she were looking past me and back into herself.

I pulled away from her plucking fingers and retreated slowly, as from a potentially dangerous dog. Sometimes I hear her voice yet, after all this time, seven years, and I can hear her saying, "What. What. What." Over and over and over.

I, too, sat in front of the TV the day it happened.

I never felt the nausea.

I never felt anything. I still don't.

One minute Connie Chung was smiling her elegant, understated smile at me, just for me, and promising to be back in a moment, and then the TV went out. The floating green numbers on the clock radio went out; even the refrigerator ceased its self-important drone.

I thought it was just another outage, and settled in to wait. How long? I don't know that either. I finally just gave up and went to bed. Funny, I brushed my teeth with orange juice. The water had smelled funny. I remembered that.

I read somewhere that the most common and terrifying nightmare is, I mean, was, of falling. The worst nightmare I ever had was of my family dying all at once and leaving me alone. I dreamed this recurrently as I grew up, and then on July 18, I woke and it was true to the two-hundred-millionth power.

The world died as I slept with orange-juice-sweetened breath.

The silence was the worst, until, of course, the people began to rot. The heat didn't help. Even on peaceful weekday mornings, after everyone had left for work, there were noises, sounds we were so used to that we didn't even notice them. Motors and currents and vibrations. Hums and buzzes and chinks. Rustlings of existence.

On July 18, there was nothing. Dear God, how much nothing there was. Connie never came back. She owed me that. To come back and tell me sleekly and sympathetically what the hell happened to my world. To our world. Even though I can't forgive her, I hope she survived too. Although, if I think of it, which I try not to do, it would probably be kinder to hope she didn't. To hope she died quickly with her microphone and makeup on.

CHAPTER 2

Nancy is trying to care for the things she calls children. Pets is more like it. I prefer to pretend that she doesn't know how much I loathe them all.

I can't believe I feel this way. I was a student teacher, an elementary school teacher, second grade, my senior-year internship.

My apartment was just two blocks from the school. It was the first time I had a place of my own. My folks' house was my base of operations during my first two years of college. I came home for holidays and laundry. I was welcome there until I brought home a special friend for the weekend and my sweet unsuspecting mom brought us a tray of coffee and orange juice (again with the orange juice) and English muffins studded with raisins.

I'd had sleepovers since I was eight and I'm sure she thought this was just another school chum. I'm very sure she did not expect us to be holding each other close with our jammie tops off, tongueing up a storm in my white canopy bed.

It is, I suppose, possible that I staged the discovery, to escape having to announce my preference for persons of the female persuasion. Persons with corresponding rather than complementary body parts.

They didn't scream and holler and demand my departure. My parents were too polite, too liberal, too loving to throw me out in the cold, although it was May and warm. They just stiffened up and distanced themselves from me, threw up defensive blockades between us. We all knew it was best if I left. I believed we would be able to be friends someday. I believed there would be a someday.

My junior year, I transferred to a small college in neighboring Michigan. The teaching internship was as perfectly timed as a stage direction. Exit Lez, stage left. Parents huddle to Fade. Curtain.

Curtain up on Apartment Interior. Lez enters, juggling boxes and bags.

I loved the apartment, my classes, and my new job. The kids were great, bright and eager as sitcom kids. Sorry, I just realized that if there is anyone ever to read this, you probably don't know what

7

sitcoms are, or maybe even my ever-lovin' orange juice and fresh fruit. Dear God, for a bunch of seedless green grapes.

Never mind, where was I? Yes, loving my apartment and teaching and the principal of Wright Street Elementary.

Martha. I want to tell you a little about Martha. She deserves that much, at least.

She was fifty-two when we met, on my first day on the job. She supervised the student teachers. She was a widow and a grandmother and a Ph.D. She was brilliant and witty and intense — and thirty-two years my senior. She drank too much, she said, but I never heard her stammer, never saw her stumble.

For seven months she made me crazy by standing too close and leaning in to talk to me. She drew me to her with eyes so dark you could not discern the pupils. She always touched me when we talked of discipline or millage or her grandkids. She brushed against me, or hugged me in a maternal, careless way. But always she briskly declined to meet me for lunch, or a show, or the half-a-hundred excuses I thought up for us to spend time together.

Finally, one day after school, alone in the lounge, we sat together over coffee. Winding down. It was the last day before spring break and the kids had been wild, practically bouncing off the walls.

Our nerves were frayed. As she talked about how her grandkids would be unable to visit for Easter, she idly traced the pattern on the ring I wore, still wear, my grandmother's. Her fingertips barely brushed my skin and I jerked my hand away.

"Don't! Don't touch me anymore!" I startled us

both by shouting. I stood abruptly and turned to dump my coffee into the sink and rinse the mug.

"Why?" she finally whispered.

"I can't bear it when you touch me. You don't mean it — do you?" I turned to accuse her, and was surprised to find her standing very near.

"You know I love you, don't you, Martha? Don't you, Mrs. Doyle?" The words I'd wanted to say for so long sounded bitter and harsh. "You do know, and you've been toying with me all this time! Is it fun? Do you like to watch me squirm with wanting you?"

I turned back to the sink, stuffing escaped pillows of sugar back into their broken-handled mug prison, and swiped vengefully at the semicircle stains on the counter.

She touched my shoulder lightly and murmured, "I do want you too. I just ... I never ... I don't know how. What to do. I have never ... Please be patient. I love you too ... dear ... darling."

I closed my eyes and savored her last words, hesitantly spoken.

I was patient, but I brought her a rose, a bracelet, a book of poems — Emily Dickinson.

I knew we would be good together. I could wait. I could wait forever to hold my Martha.

I thought we had time.

I thought there would be a *we*.

CHAPTER 3

Nancy was angry with me for days after I suggested that she let her "children" run around outside without any pants on so she won't have to spend all her time scraping shit off their bodies. Just fill the yard with children shit and chicken shit.

Chickens. That's all she talked about when we met. Half crazy and muttering mostly incoherently, she said, "Chickens. There will be chickens. I have to get some. Chickens."

"I had a dream," she said, "and I have to get some chickens."

It was the same day I backed away from the woman all gray. I knew I had to get out of the city. It was starting to stink and also, I began to think maybe it was just here. Maybe somewhere else people still fought over the comics page or whose turn it was for dishes. The plumbing had kept working, but the water had an acrid smell, and I thought it might be the source of the problem. I still couldn't figure out why all the electrical circuits shut down. I thought they were all automated.

There was a full tank of gas in my old Cutlass, but it wouldn't have mattered. There were plenty of cars around to choose from. Although I might have had to look for the keys in some rather nasty places.

I headed west, through downtown. People hadn't just died in the comfort of their homes. There were bodies everywhere, like a B movie of the '50s. I kept expecting someone to yell "CUT" and everybody to get up, rearrange their hair and clothes and go home. Except, of course, they stunk and were beginning to bloat in the unsympathetic July sun.

Martha was in England with her daughter. I missed her. I was afraid for her. I guess I'll never know if she survived.

As I drove slowly through the maze of illegally parked vehicles I heard an almost electrical buzz. I turned my car radio off and on a couple of times before I realized that the sound was the collective song of a city of ecstatic flies. A giant block party for flies. Bring Your Own Body. So flies survived. No surprise to me. Rats were scurrying along beside buildings. The real survivors: rats and flies.

Our library was Number 3 of the Proposed Designs for Municipal Buildings, duplicated in dozens of cities right down to the location of the *Reader's Guide to Periodic Literature.* Our school had conducted its yearly pilgrimage to give honor to the Dewey Decimal System. The librarian had dutifully posted, for one week only, the thank-you notes from the deeply grateful studentry.

As I approached the library, it occurred to me that all the knowledge and wisdom and insight contained in those 250,421 volumes was useless without readers. That all the writing of all the ages was useless and possibly dangerous. No doubt learning had led my fair city to becoming Purina Fly Food.

I toyed briefly with the thought of burning the damn thing down when I saw a girl skipping down the steps with her arms full of books and a sheaf of red cotton-candy hair floating back from her head.

She was muttering to herself and almost smiling. I stopped and called to her.

"Hey you!" Great opening line, eh?

She skip-stepped up to the window and said, "Chickens. There will be chickens. I have to get some. Chickens."

Her eyes were an incredible light blue and almost transparent, as if there were a light shining through from the inside.

I assumed the light was insanity, and who could blame her?

Up close I could see that she was not twelve or

thirteen, as I had first guessed. There were lines at the corners of her eyes, the kind delicate skin collects. And there were dark smudges under her eyes. Her features were sharp and she had a sprinkle of freckles across her nose.

That wild red hair dominated — hair that shunned well-meaning advice from combs and brushes. I had an insane desire to grab a handful to see if it would crackle or snap.

She did not move away from the car, but stood clutching that stack of books to her childlike body.

Blue-veined fingers kept time to nonexistent music. She didn't speak again, but seemed to be waiting. I had not studied my lines; I did not know what to say.

Finally, she said again, "Chickens, I have to get some."

So I said, "Well, get in then, we'll find some."

We drove out of the city. She had piled the books on the seat between us so she could fasten her seat belt.

I almost laughed, or cried. I looked at the books as I drove — not much traffic in a city of dead people. Here and there were pile-ups or cars crashed into light poles. The drivers must have died at the wheel.

Nancy's books were all about chickens — *How to Raise Chickens, Chickens for Fun and Profit,* that sort of thing. There was a children's book on the bottom, *The Little Red Hen.*

The light was still there behind her eyes. It

should have been insanity, but I was to learn that it was worse.

Much worse.

It was hope.

CHAPTER 4

How could a grief-stricken, shocked young woman have known there would be chickens?

People died, cats and dogs died. I have never seen another mosquito; maybe they are all dead too. Cats and mosquitoes and men seemed to be gone. The few scurrying or hunched human figures we saw seemed all to be female zombies.

We played a game as if we were children, antsy to be home from a long car ride. Except instead of license plates from Massachusetts, or red Renaults, we scored ten points for any signs of life.

She had thirty points and I only had ten when we left Jackson's city limits. The light was fading rapidly in a cobblestone sky. A cool breeze seduced away the stench of the decomposing city.

Soon fat raindrops committed gleeful suicide on the windshield.

"So, what did you do before, chicken lady?" I asked.

But she was asleep, just like that, with her head back against the headrest and her mouth open slightly. Her fragile-looking hands twitched occasionally. It seemed as if that spooky light shone even through her lids

As I glanced over at her again, I saw one solitary tear trickle slowly down her pale cheek.

That one damn tear hammered out my fate. It and it alone was responsible for everything that has happened since. All of it.

I had given up any chance of motherhood with the realization that the only thing I wanted boys to do to me in the back seats of their daddies' cars was what a girl could do to me, only more gently and with clean fingernails and smooth faces.

But all the maternal instincts I would ever feel were born in the pain of that one distilled tear. I knew I had to take care of this child-woman. I had to protect her and find her chickens.

When she woke up, I tried another tack. "So, what's your name?"

"What's yours?"

I was tempted to say, "I asked you first," but just told her my name, my nickname.

"Vic," I said. I suddenly wanted Martha's voice to be the last to call me by my full name.

"Oh, I have an uncle by that name, or did have ... I don't know ..."

"You didn't tell me yours," I prompted.

"Nancy. My name is Nancy."

"Hi, Nancy," I smiled my first-day-of-school smile, hoping it would work as well with her as with second-graders.

"Tell me about your chickens," I urged, show-and-tellish. "Have you always had chickens?"

"Is everybody dead?" Nancy's face went a little slack. The smudges were even darker under her eyes.

"I don't know, hon." Did I sound consoling or condescending? The *hon* just slipped out, an improper proper noun standing cold and naked. But if she noticed it, she didn't seem to mind.

"All my people died," she said, and told me how it was for her in that flat, matter-of-fact monotone that worried me.

"I don't know about my family," I offered, choking up. But it was Martha's face I saw, Martha's short blond hair, coarse and willful. Her raw-boned, post-athletic body. Her purposeful stride down halls too small for her abilities. Why had I not gone to Martha's house? Why hadn't I waited for her? What if she returned from England? Alive? Why was I driving away from destruction with a total stranger instead of waiting for the woman I loved?

A ghastly slide show performed itself in my mind. Those bloated caricatures of human beings with Martha's dear face superimp\sed on each one. I could not bear to see her dead. I would rather live hoping she survived than see her fly-pecked.

"Are we going to die?" Nancy's voice broke through my grieving reverie.

"I don't know. I don't know anything. But I would guess not. I feel okay. I think whatever it was takes you out right away or not at all. The water smelled funny. Maybe we have better immune systems. I don't know."

"I still don't get it. Why not us?"

I lost my temper suddenly, snarling, "I don't goddamnit know. What am I? Consumer Information, Pueblo, Colorado?"

Nancy shrank into the corner, stunned and silent.

I murmured, "I'm sorry. Really. This is hard for me too."

Neither of us spoke for many miles until Nancy shouted, "Stop! Stop the car! Listen! Do you hear? Listen."

She was smiling radiantly, a latter-day visionary straining for the voices of angels?

"Chickens!" she crowed, like one of them. "It's chickens!"

We drove up a long unpaved driveway to a farmhouse perched on the false promise of a hill.

"There sure as hell are chickens," I boasted, as if responsible for her true prophecy.

She turned to me and said, very seriously, "You ought to watch your language, you know. Swearing isn't really necessary." Then she unbuckled her seat belt, stepped out of the car and over a denim-overalled body.

"Let's see if we can find anything to eat." She declared, "I'm starving."

And I was going to take care of *her*?

"You go look through the house," Nancy commanded. "See if there's anyone else here. I'll find us something to eat."

"What about the old man?"

"I don't think he's hungry." Nancy grinned.

"I won't be either, until we bury him. Maybe you noticed the aroma?"

"I suppose you're right. Do you know how?"

"Well, I never took a class in impromptu burial, but I don't suppose it's that complicated," I said, already on my way to the garage, the most logical place to find a shovel. Or two.

We both dug, gagging, but even with two, we couldn't get down as deep as we probably should have. But since there was no one to tell us how badly we were doing it, we dug until we couldn't anymore. We dug a grave right there in the front yard, and as the sun set we rolled the body, two days dead and rotting, into it. Something glinted with the last rays of light, and I bent to pick up a pair of wire-rimmed glasses. I tossed them into the grave and then we covered it all over.

We were exhausted as we stumbled up rickety side porch steps and into the kitchen.

"Hello!" Nancy called, "Anybody here?"

There was only a musty hollow echo for answer.

Nancy started rummaging through kitchen

cupboards, saying, "I'll get dinner, you go look through the house."

There wasn't much light left, and I didn't have much energy, so I made a minimal search. It was a sad, empty house, huge, with five bedrooms and two parlors, a full basement, full attic, two sets of stairs — one discreetly positioned at the back of the house, for servants, no doubt. Odd to think this ramshackle shell had once housed servants, probably a family. It felt as if no one had lived or loved in this house for a long time. No one but our white-haired and buried host. I hurried back to Nancy and "dinner."

She found some candles and had melted their bottoms onto the top of an enormous white stove. She also found jars of canned fruit. The gas was still working, but we didn't know for how long, and Nancy didn't trust the food left in the refrigerator. So we each had our own jar of peaches and packets of Saltines and ate them by candlelight.

Nancy cut her peaches with the side of her spoon, eating daintily and sipping the juice fastidiously.

This enraged me for absolutely no reason and I slurped mine greedily out of the jar, deliberately stuffing whole peach halves into my mouth with the crackers. The juice dribbled onto my shirt as I realized that I had not eaten since all this began and that my hands were black with grave dirt. I was wondering if it was unlucky to eat grave dirt when Nancy said, "Do you think it's safe to eat this stuff?"

I almost laughed. "Dirt? I don't think dirt will hurt us."

She looked confused, having not read my mind after all. "No, peaches."

"You can just call me Vic."

"What?"

She was getting more confused, and I was getting the slap-happies total exhaustion brings. I tried to be serious.

"If we don't eat something we're going to die anyway, so why not?"

It was hardly reassuring, but all I could think to say. Besides, it was late. My jar was empty, Nancy's nearly so, and the crackers devoured.

Nancy conscientiously locked the back door behind us as we went upstairs. I claimed the first room at the top of the stairs for my own, leaving Nancy to make her own decision about where to sleep. I was too tired and filthy to suggest anything more companionable. I would have gladly traded my left tit for a hot shower, a long hot shower, but I hadn't yet checked the water supply, and I was grateful for the dusty quilt-covered bed. I didn't even remove my shoes.

I heard the springs in the next room squeal a welcome.

Just as I fell asleep, I heard a whimper and a sob, but I don't know if it was Nancy or me.

CHAPTER 5

"Are there many more of these jars of fruit?" I slurped down another jar of peaches along with some dry oatmeal for breakfast. Nancy had pears.

"Some, but they won't last long."

"We'll take them with us." I was ready to move on.

Nancy wasn't.

"Take them where?" she asked, pear syrup dripping off her chin.

"Wherever we're going next."

"Not we."

"What do you mean?"

"I'm staying right here."

"For what?" I had known her for less than twenty-four hours, yet it was inconceivable that she would not want to come with me.

"There are chickens."

"Fuck the chickens. You haven't even looked at the damn chickens since we got here."

"I don't care. I only had to come here. That's all I know. It was a dream. A dream told me to find chickens. I'm staying."

"Lady, you are fucking crazy, you know that? Chickens, dreams, do you do everything your damn dreams tell you to? That's nuts!"

"Some dreams need to be obeyed. You have to know which ones. I knew this was one of them."

"What's here for you? Chickens?" I lost my temper. I couldn't help it. "Chickens and chicken shit and dreams and dream shit. You stupid little bitch, you'll starve to death or die of thirst!"

"No I won't." Her calm assurance was infuriating.

"Don't tell me — you had another dream, right? Voices and visions, what next, St. Nancy?"

"I got up early."

"Congratulations. Double sainthood for sure."

"I looked around."

"Christopher fucking Columbus!"

"There's water here."

"What?"

"Water. There's water."

"So what? The water in the city was bad. For all we know, it might have been the problem. Or part of it."

"I know that, but this is *well* water." Nancy stood

and calmly took me by my grimy hand. She led me out to the back yard where an assortment of ancient farm equipment serenely fulfilled its destiny by rusting to extinction. The rust was the color of her hair. I wondered again what would happen if I clutched a handful. Would it stain?

Behind a valiantly struggling lilac tree she motioned a classic "Tah dah!"

"It's a water pump," I said.

"It works."

The concrete block surrounding the pump was splashed with water, and a bucket stood half full under its spout. The water was clear, too, I saw, not cloudy.

Nancy proudly said, "I had to prime it."

"Prime it?"

"Yeah, pour some water down it to get it going. My grandpa showed me how. He had a farm too."

"Where did you get the water to prime it?"

"Out of the water heater in the basement. There's lots of water in that. But now we can just save a little every time we draw some and keep it for priming."

"It works?" I squatted down and smelled it. There was none of the acrid odor I'd noticed in the city.

"Yup. I think maybe the old guy used it regular. Maybe he liked the old ways. Grandpa did."

"Regularly," I corrected her. "You know, if there's water in the heater, it's probably well water. We could each have a shower. Only one, but I could sure use it."

She grinned. "That sounds great! Guess what else I found?" She led me to another treasure, around the other side of the house.

24

More lilacs, only this time a huge healthy copse of them, with a distinct path beaten into it.

"It's an outhouse." Nancy gestured her tah dah again.

"I see that."

"He used it too, there's fresh paper inside."

"Great. It stinks. Can't we just use the toilet and pour water down it after?"

"Sure, if you want to haul water all day long. I don't."

I was beginning to think I liked her better when she was childlike and helpless. This resourcefulness was a surprise.

"How about that shower?" Nancy chirped. "You can go first."

I hated to admit to her how I longed for a hot shower, even if it was my last one. "Why me first? You found the water."

"You need it worse!" She laughed as she ran to the house.

It didn't take a whole lot to persuade me. I followed her inside.

Nancy found a bar of Fels Naphtha soap, a thin, stiff towel, and faded but clean shirt and jeans.

"These should almost fit," she said.

"His?"

"Yeah, I guess. They're stiff because they were dried in the sun. Smell." She shoved the clothes into my face. "Better than fabric softener, huh? Vic . . . is that for Victoria?"

Her conversational switches startled me. I just nodded, then added, "Just Vic, okay?"

Nancy sat down on the edge of the tub and wrapped her arms around her knees. It seems odd that, realizing she meant to keep me company while I bathed, I was hesitant to undress in front of her. After all, being naked with another woman was one of my favorite pastimes. Maybe I was still thinking of her as a child. I hesitated, feeling foolish, but knowing I would feel more foolish asking her to leave. I undressed and washed as she chatted, paying no attention to my nudity, my erect nipples. The air was cold after the heat of the water.

Smiling, she said, "There's wood, too."

"Wood?"

"Wood. Like for the fireplaces and wood stove."

"Wood stove?" I felt as if I were trying to learn a new language. Repeat after me ... I shook my head. "But there's a working gas line."

"But it won't last, will it? Besides, there's a gas stove. And bottled gas. I don't know how to use a wood stove to cook on, but we can figure it out. And if we can get some tanks of gas and figure out how to hook them up, we can use the gas stove when the natural gas runs out."

Listening to Nancy prattle on about cooking and washing and heating as I dried my hair, I almost forgot my decision to leave. I finished buttoning the old man's shirt around me — not a bad fit — and said, "What about food? What are you going to eat?"

"We, Vic, you mean *we*, don't you? What are *we* going to eat?"

"Nancy," I said, looking into her see-through eyes, "I can't stay here."

"Why? Why not?"

"I just can't." I turned to avoid watching the tears collect in those damned incredible eyes.

"But why? We have everything we need. We'll be okay. Why won't you stay?"

"I have to know. I have to see if there are any more people. I have to know what happened, and if it happened everywhere. Maybe it's just here. I need to find out why."

"What about me?" she whispered, one tear escaping her struggle for control.

For an eternal second, the urge was unbearably strong to gently brush away her tear, to take her in my arms, to stay. I felt that if only I could hold her, I could stay forever. I was startled to realize that I wanted her, and was suddenly ashamed. My radar had not signaled that she was like me, that she felt that for me. And Martha. Had I forgotten her so quickly? And what of my maternal resolution to care for Nancy, protect her? Did caring include seduction?

Confusion and disgust drove me to push past Nancy and head angrily toward the kitchen.

She repeated her plaintive, "What about me?"

"You'll be all right," I shouted. "You've got your fucking chickens!"

I made it to the car, slamming myself in. The keys dangled where I had left them, a foolish habit before, sensible now.

As I drove away I heard her yell, "You watch your language!"

CHAPTER 6

Not twelve miles from the farm, I began to notice more houses that were closer together, but no signs of life. It didn't register that I didn't actually see any bodies.

The Jefferson town-limit sign boasted a population of 11,500, and announced monthly meetings of the Lions Club and Knights of Columbus. I smiled bitterly. I doubted these claims now.

There was a small shopping mall just past the sign and I pulled into the parking lot. A grocery store, a discount department store and a Radio Shack dominated the plaza, with a pizzeria and Photo Mart wedged in. I parked at the grocery store, walking up to and into the doors. I expected them to swing open at my approach.

Laughing at my own foolishness, I pushed hard to enter. There was the nasty stench of rotten meat, deli food and spoiled veggies.

It was incredibly eerie in there, dark and quiet, no cash registers, demanding children or Muzak. The clinking wheels on the cart I chose echoed through the silent building.

Strolling leisurely, I filled the cart with jars and cans and whatever of the fresh fruit hadn't turned bad. Peanut butter, tuna fish. I tried to think what to choose, but ended up just piling stuff in. I tore open a bag of potato chips and finished my shopping quickly. The meat department made an instant vegetarian of me.

It should have occurred to me that there were no bodies in the store either; dead chuck roasts were the worst things I met.

Bagging my own groceries, the bizarre nature of it all made me empty all the racks of Juicy Fruit gum into my bags. I giggled with nervous guilt. No one minded. No one asked me to pay. Pay whom? With what?

I thought I saw movement as I drove through town, what was left of it, but decided it was wishful thinking. Is a town still a town if no one lives there anymore? Or nearly no one. How many people does it take to make a town?

The sense of loss, the loneliness, was almost a taste. For the first time since it happened, I began to comprehend the enormity of a dead world, or country, or state. Or just this one little Michigan town, proud of its hundred dozen citizens. Somehow this small town seemed emptier than my own home had been.

I remembered all the times I longed to escape humanity. I dreamed vacations to "get away from it all." We all did. My friends would yell at one another to shut up and to drop dead. We complained about the loss of privacy. Dear God.

Back in my car, I practically idled through town, memorizing the stores, open now forever, and closed forever too. No more free delivery. I passed a school, an elementary school. A bright red dirt bike, the envy of grades K–6, was propped against a tree.

I parked at the curb and sobbed, screaming hysterically until I felt the numbness return. I wanted to forget it all — the children, my family, Martha, Nancy, everyone. I was suddenly, insanely jealous of everyone who had died. Whatever power or random factor left me alive had done me no favor. I wondered if it was really possible to die of heartbreak. It was hard to breathe.

In my freshman year of college, I wrote a dreadful poem based on the theory that no matter what horrific method we chose to destroy our race, the universe would be as oblivious to our final cry of despair as a bored ex-lover. *Ho-hum, are you quite finished?* she would yawn. *I do have more important things to do, you know.*

I turned the car around, stopping once more, loading silver canisters into the trunk.

I knew how to hook up bottled gas, damn it! *My* grandfather had lived in a trailer park!

* * * * *

Nancy didn't even have the grace to fake surprise
at my same-day return, although I thought her eyes
were swollen and red-rimmed.

She smiled at the groceries, asking, "Did you get
toothbrushes? Toilet paper? Maxi pads?"

Of course I hadn't, but there were three jars of
pickled pig's feet.

"I'll make you a list next time."

"I have to figure out how many trips I have left
in the tank." It occurred to me on the way home
that the car wouldn't run forever.

"Tell me about the town," she said as she
arranged the food on the shelves. She'd spent the
time I was gone making the kitchen her own:
cleaning, rearranging, and throwing away — black
plastic garbage bags were piled at the back door.

"I can't tell how many survived. Not many, I
would guess. It's a small town, one good-sized
grocery store, several party stores, a discount
department store, two hardwares, feed store, chiro-
practor, gift shop, drugstore, and three pizza
parlors."

"Three?"

"Yup, and get this — four churches, one bar.
Didn't seem to help any, did it?" I scoffed.

Nancy spun to face me, her spine rigid and eyes
blazing indignation. "I imagine it helped them a
great deal." She spoke carefully, as if to keep from
losing her temper. Her face was so beautiful in its
righteous rage, I could have kissed her.

To break the tension I said, "Hey, I didn't tell
you the best part."

It was my turn to lead her by the hand, deceptively fragile, to the car trunk. As I unlocked it, I said, "Make a wish, Nance."

Smiling, she closed her eyes. "Pepperoni pizza."

"Close — bottled gas." My turn to tah dah.

Damned if she didn't throw her arms around me and hug me like a kid. Damned if I didn't hug her back. She smelled of Fels Naphtha soap, even her hair. I was awed at her fragility. I thought of Emily Dickinson describing herself "like a wren." It had been a long time since I had held anyone that small in my arms, except an occasional knee-scraped or name-called kid.

I held Nancy close, burying my face in those crackling flames of sweet-smelling hair, still damp. It didn't snap or stain, it yielded under my caress, scarring me for life.

I felt *I love you* gathering in my mouth and clenched my teeth to prevent escape. Frightened of her rejection, I pushed her away and lifted the fat silver capsules from the trunk.

"Where do you want these babies, ma'am?" I joked, an odd euphoria rising within me.

Maybe Nancy would want me someday. Maybe if I was patient.

That was how quickly we fell into our roles. Stereotypical to boot. Nancy took care of the house, cleaning room by room with a bucket of cold water at her feet. Nancy did the cooking, too, but we did the dishes together. We had yet to tackle doing laundry in pots of water heated on the stove. We'd had no problem with the gas, but I split wood to stack for winter anyway. The old man had done the same. There was a pile of logs all ready for me. I tried not to think what I would have to do when there was no more gas and the wood was gone. Tree-chopping was another course not offered by my alma mater.

Nancy was experimenting with the wood stove, even though I had successfully hooked up the gas tanks. And it seemed I was to become the hunter-gatherer, woman-directed. Future anthropologists take note. If there are future anthropologists. If there are future anythings.

Nancy was preparing for the initial test of possible futures. She came to me with a shopping list. First on the list were tampons.

"It's about that time," she said, blushing. "That is, if there is still a time. I mean, if nothing's changed." She seemed embarrassed, as if she'd forgotten I was a woman and would need tampons, too.

"What difference will it make if we don't have periods?" I challenged. "I can chop your wood, but I can't give you babies. What if there aren't any men? What if they all died? Frankly, I wouldn't mind not having to deal with the smell and the mess of menstruation anymore."

Nancy looked at me with an expression of total incomprehension and then said, "Smell and mess — that reminds me. We need lime too, to pour down the outhouse hole." And she scribbled it on the list.

Nancy went with me into town that one time, but never again. The reality disturbed her. Quiet almost all the way home, she finally said, "I guess I'd rather pretend we chose to live out here, like this. I keep thinking we could stop any time we want to, but we just prefer it this way. I don't want to see that dead town anymore. I want to go on pretending. Forever. It will be forever, won't it?"

I couldn't answer. Like a scream in an empty school, my silence hung in what little space was left in my overloaded car.

I didn't tell Nancy, God knows why, about the changes I'd noticed in the town. Small changes, but perceptible. The spoiled meats and fruits had been removed from the grocery store, and there were fewer goods on the shelves, though still plenty. All the jars of pig's feet were gone. Even with unmowed lawns and haphazardly parked cars, the town seemed neater. But I had to put the town and its eerie changes out of my mind in order to deal with a week of Nancy's weeping and temper tantrums. The tension broke finally in a tidal wave of blood. Nancy's period was accompanied by hours of excruciating cramps, mine with the slightest of backaches. My black mood began the same hour as Nancy's release.

CHAPTER 7

Time is one of the many things we lost. Neither of us wore a watch, and there were no mechanical clocks in the farmhouse. We knew day from night, but could only guess at the time. I suppose I could have gotten a watch at the drugstore, but after a while, knowing the hour seemed inconsequential. We rose with the sun, ate lunch at what we still called noon, when the sun was more or less overhead, and went to bed not long after sundown. We weren't sure what the day of the week was; we hadn't kept track. Our bodies marked the months, and seasonal changes remained. It was just odd sometimes not to know 9:15 or 11:11, or Thursday.

Garbage service too. Just take it out to the curb on Tuesday morning and forget it. That's how it had been. Now I pile cans out behind the decrepit barn. Garbage I bury. There isn't much paper trash, no newspapers or junk mail, you know, but what there is I burn in a rusted trash drum. Tampons we drop down the outhouse hole which is sprinkled weekly with lime. Though I'd seen rats in the city, I hadn't yet spotted any on the farm. And I didn't want to.

There was no TV or radio, but I found dozens of boxes of books in the huge attic. Nothing published after 1922, but I didn't mind. In school, I'd taken mostly contemporary lit classes. This was my chance to expand. There was Emerson, Thoreau, Shakespeare, Poe, Montaigne, Dickens and my old pal Emily Dickinson, which I took to my room in a fit of morbidity. I even struggled through a stack of penny dreadfuls and found them true to their name.

There was an odd book packed in with the classics. Red. Newer. The title: *Moments Together*. The author's name on the spine matched that on all the mail we'd thrown out — the old man we'd buried shallowly in his own front yard, our front yard.

Curious, I opened the book to find 350 blank pages. The only writing was on the flyleaf. Hand-written, it said, "Grandpa, Just do it, it's never too late. Love, Stacy." I sat with that blank book on my lap for a long time before I placed it carefully back into its box, sorry to have found it.

There was an old family Bible which I brought

down to Nancy. I thought she would like it, and she rewarded me with a rare hug. I wanted to give her the world — as it had been, of course.

I would have done anything for her, given her anything, except I began to suspect that the only thing she really wanted was the only thing that was totally impossible.

There were damn few eggs deposited by those chickens, and Nancy had been feeding them to us. But then she began studying up on chickens in those books she had taken out of the library, now seriously overdue. Nancy started talking to them, and to me about them. She wanted to coop them at night and provide a better diet than the bugs they scratched up for themselves. She added chicken feed to our next supply list. I wondered how long it would be before she let some hatch.

It would be a type of test. She asked for vegetable seeds, too. Another test.

Nancy solved the problem of having to siphon gas.

"Why don't you just trade in? There are lots of cars to choose from."

Her sweet reasonableness sometimes delighted, sometimes infuriated me. She saw things more clearly, found solutions more quickly than I did. But her resourcefulness was a constant reminder that my vow to take care of her was unfulfillable. It was more often a case of her taking care of me. I became determined to find a way. I vowed to find a way to keep my vow.

* * * * *

37

Premenstrual syndrome and a thunderstorm brought Nancy to my bed late one night.

She stood in the doorway and sniffed. "Can I crawl in with you for a while?" She wore an old-fashioned, voluminous nightgown she'd found in a drawer. Grandma's?

Ever the parody, I wore the old man's cotton pajamas. Our nightclothes had probably slept together before.

Struggling to contain my joy, I welcomed her with ridicule. " 'Fraidy cat, scared of a little thunder and lightning? Come on in, silly."

I cradled her in my arms as if I had done so a hundred times. If dreams count, I had. Relishing the storm as a visual orgasm of nature, I was touched by Nancy's fear.

"I'm scared, Vic. Oh God, I'm scared," Nancy whimpered.

"It's just a storm, baby, just a storm. It'll be over soon." I hoped I was soothing her, but I was not soothed by her nearness. I could smell the crude soap she insisted on using, though I'd brought home better.

"It isn't just the storm. It isn't. It's everything. I want my life back. I want TV and movies and the telephone. I want my family." She was sobbing. I held her closer, rocking her instinctively.

"We are family now, Nance. We're all we've got."

"God, Vic, I don't want to die like this. I don't want to lie dead in the yard."

"Nancy, darling, don't. You'll make yourself sick." I was startled to hear my mother's voice coming out of my mouth.

Nancy burrowed closer to me. I could feel her wrenlike boniness and felt my own sudden flush of desire. I stroked her face, tracing the delicate features and wiping away her tears. I teased her about playing connect-the-dot with her freckles, and she smiled a little. I smoothed her hair away from her face, toying with the curling tendrils at her temples. I watched her pulse throb there until I thought my heart beat in time with hers.

With parted fingers I combed her rust-colored hair, down past her shoulder, down her back. I rubbed her shoulder and massaged the back of her neck with my free hand, still stroking her wonderful cascade of hair.

My hand trailed down and I massaged the small of her back.

And the whole time I murmured comforting endearments.

Dear.

Darling.

Sweet.

Angel.

Her breathing was calmer and warm on my neck. It felt so close, so right. I was moving my hand around her waist, aching to cup her tiny breasts. I almost sobbed with desire.

"I love you," I whispered. "I love you so much."

The forbidden words were the right ones at exactly the right moment.

"Oh Vic," she whispered. "I love you, too. I want us to be together forever."

"Yes, oh yes, Nancy." I choked, my eyes filling with tears, with gratitude, with love. "Forever." I moved slightly, to kiss her pale cheek, her lips. But she pulled away and looked up at me with gleaming eyes that seemed almost turquoise in the light of the retreating lightning.

"Yes," Nancy whispered. "Forever. Even after life. That's why I have to know." She hesitated.

"Know what? That I love you?"

"No. If ... if ... you're baptized."

"If I'm *what*?"

"Baptized. I am. When I was little. If we die here together and you're not baptized we won't be together anymore. I couldn't stand that. If you're not, we could do it tomorrow. We could do it at the pump."

Well, what the hell was I supposed to say to that? *No, I'm not baptized, but I sure would like to make love to you? Baptize me with your tongue, baby? Baptize, shmaptize, I want to own, possess, and eat you?*

Of course not. Not with that pure light shining from the inside out of her. I lay on my back, staring at the ceiling as she jabbered on about the importance of my baptism. Finally, I laughed until I cried. I laughed at myself and Nancy and whatever god thought it would be amusing to throw us together. St. Nancy and the dyke. What a combination!

Nancy started to cry again. She must have thought I was making fun of her. So I reassured her, shooed her to her own bed, and let her baptize me the next morning at the pump. It didn't hurt at all and it made her happy. God, she looked beautiful.

*　*　*　*　*

Nancy wanted yarn and knitting needles. She added them to the list of what we figured would be the last run of the Cutlass.

"When I get back we'll have a new car. Got any preferences?"

"Blue," Nancy smiled. "And blue yarn. Don't forget. I wrote down everything you need to look for."

"Damnit, woman, do I look stupid to you?" I pretended annoyance as I drove off.

"And watch your language!" she scolded behind me.

I smiled to myself. Her vulgarity-scolding and my grammar-correcting had become a comfortable routine, an almost marital ritual. I loved it, swearing sometimes deliberately to rile her righteous indignation.

I went straight to the department store. The town was beginning to feel familiar, like my own. Even the slight changes, which scared me and enticed me, and which testified to the presence of others whom I had never seen, did not dispel my feelings of proprietorship.

I was trying to decipher Nancy's preferred needle sizes, just deciding to simply take one pair of each size when a voice said, "You knit?"

I think I screamed.

Spinning around, I confronted a woman even taller than I was, and more than half again my weight. Chopped-off mousy brown hair, going gray. Heavy, lined face and crinkled blue eyes laughed at me, as did every inch of her body, it seemed.

"Sorry," she boomed, "I didn't mean to scare you. Shit. I'm real sorry." But she kept laughing. "Shit," she said. "I'm Jane."

"Jane," I repeated, terrified yet curious. She didn't look like a Jane.

"Jane's your name, too?"

"No, it's Vic. You just don't look like a Jane."

"Well, hell, it wasn't always. Used to be Bertha. Godawfullest name, Bertha. I always hated it. You ever try to change your name when everybody knows goddamn well you're Bertha?"

Nancy's voice echoed somewhere inside my head — *Watch your language!* — and I smiled, my fear ebbing.

"Shit, it's good to be whoever you want, ain't it?"

"You live here?" I asked cautiously.

"Hell yes, always have. Born here. I mean *right* here. My folks got bought out by this store. The house was right here. I figure we're standing in the bedroom right now."

"Sounds like a good place to be," I answered.

My good-time Geiger counter was on overdrive. If it was wrong, which it never had been, the remark could indicate mere weariness. But if it was right . . . I suddenly ached to be touched.

Bertha/Jane beamed. "Best goddamn place in the world. Shall we?"

My laughter echoed through the empty store. I felt myself relax, trusting her. I thought she meant right there, and began unbuttoning my shirt.

"Whoa, honey, whoa. Not here. Let's go to my place. Just a couple doors over."

She didn't give me time to be embarrassed, saying, "Been a while for you too, huh?"

"Too long." I was still laughing, "Too goddamn long."

Anonymous sex has never been my style. But I did need someone and Bertha/Jane seemed like instant old buddy.

Her house was a joyously rumpled mess, but I didn't look around too much. We went straight to her bedroom and straight to work. Her pendulous breasts and wide hips seemed just fine to me. She never apologized for the mess her house was in, or for her body. I liked that immensely.

She was talented and tender but somehow masterful at the same time. It was a lovely change from being pickle-jar-opener, top-shelf-reacher.

I chuckled at a memory.

"Tell me," Jane commanded.

"I just remembered something my last lover said to a man in a bar. We were being openly affectionate, and he barged up and demanded to know, 'Which one of you is the man?' He was obviously threatened by women who had no use for the center of his universe. Sara looked him straight in the eye, and said, 'Neither. That's the point.' Then we walked out hand-in-hand. He just stood there."

"That's beautiful." Bertha/Jane smiled. "What happened to you and Sara? A woman like that's worth keeping."

"I wanted to. She didn't. When she left she said, 'Nothing nullifies the verb *to want* as fast as *to have*.'"

"You miss her a lot."

"Actually! I haven't thought of her in ages." Then, as if some vocal dam burst, I told Bertha/Jane things I never told anyone.

I told her about Martha, and Nancy, especially about Nancy. I told her about Sara, and our sleep-over at my parents, how Sara felt used and left me for a man — a double insult. I told her about my induction to dykedom.

"The first time was with my high school gym teacher, Miss Janine Jackson. I was a senior. She was a dyke. I was curious; she was great. I got an A in Phys Ed."

Bertha/Jane chuckled appreciatively.

"What about you?" I asked.

She stretched on the crowded bed and propped herself up on one elbow. "I'm forty-three," she said. "I was married for seventeen of them years to a good man. Might have been the last one. I was a good wife. I cooked and cleaned and mended. I gave him anything he wanted any time he wanted, and he did the same for me. I couldn't have kids," she said, tracing an old white hysterectomy scar, "but we had a good life. Then one day he just popped off. His heart stopped as he was sitting on the toilet. Musta been one helluva shit."

"I'm sorry," I murmured.

"Why? Did you do it?"

She grinned sardonically. "Anyway, after the funeral, his sister the screaming dyke dragged me into the bedroom. Shut the door. Pushed me onto the bed, and did me, right there with their parents and the priest in the next room chomping tuna casserole and platitudes."

"She raped you?"

"Shit no. I didn't put up no fight. She always did intrigue me. I got off for the first time in my life. Shit, scared me silly. Didn't know what it was.

Thought I was dyin' too. Always wondered if that was incest."

"Where is she now?" Thoughtless, stupid question.

"Dead. Dead with the rest of them. But we had a good time for a while. A real good time. You up to another good time yourself?"

It was nearly dark when we finally rolled out of bed.

Back at the store, I hurriedly grabbed sackfuls of yarn and dozens of needles as Bertha/Jane scouted out my new car from the many to choose from in the parking lot.

She kissed me heartily on the mouth.

As I drove off she bellowed, "You hurry back now, and I do mean hurry."

Neither the car nor the yarn were blue. I didn't get anything else on the list, and I most certainly did not tell Nancy what I'd done in town all day.

CHAPTER 8

We wintered fairly well the first year. It was quite mild. The only protective measures we took for the chickens was to move them into the garage, which had thick concrete-block walls.

We bathed less, often heating water in a huge canning kettle on top of the stove. The natural gas lines held up. Then together we would lift and pour the hot water into a large washtub we found in the basement. It was easier than hauling it to the bathtub. We started by adding cold water to boiling, but Nancy figured out that by only heating it to the right temperature, we would save time and work.

We took turns bathing. It seemed like too much work for two baths in one day. The tub was large, but I still had to stand or kneel. Nancy could sit down with her knees pulled up to her chin. Sometimes I tortured myself by pulling up a chair to talk to her as she methodically soaped and rinsed. Sometimes I offered to scrub her back. Sometimes she let me. It gave me something to dream about.

Once I asked her what she wanted, planning to brazenly confess my own dreams, if she asked. But she hadn't read the script my imagination had authored. She simply answered, "Chicks hatching and a vegetable garden. I want to be weeding a vegetable garden."

She plotted and replotted her garden-to-be as I read the winter away. We also passed a wrenching week or two sorting through the previous owner's personal effects, burning some, storing the rest in the attic.

We seemed to finally accept our situation as probably permanent, not a transition, as we had first figured, or as I had first figured.

The house was ours, we knew that. No one was going to challenge our claim, and the payments were well within our budget. Possession bought our legacy.

Our luck with the gas lines ended in early December, from lack of repairs, we decided. So I hauled in firewood and water. Nancy fed the chickens, cooked and cleaned. We were the perfect couple. We even fought.

"You said we would need more wood *soon*. You didn't say we needed it this very fucking minute! Get off my back!"

The only thing lacking was conjugal rights.

I would have been okay, maybe, if I hadn't met Bertha/Jane. But thoughts of her ample body, warm and waiting in town, often drove me nearly nuts.

I made do with a variation of the five-finger exercise and a cunningly carved walking stick I found in the front hall closet.

Often, I fantasized about seducing Nancy. She had no tits to speak of, but I wanted them as much as I wanted Bertha/Jane's huge ones. I felt guilty for wanting Nancy, and I felt guilty for having had Bertha/Jane. Then I got mad at feeling guilty and took it out on Nancy. Her hurt vulnerability made me want her more. Which made me feel guilty. Ad nauseam.

Sometimes, instead of being hurt, she would snap back, but her short-lived furies were even more effective at arousing me.

Nancy chose a day to call Christmas. The only calendar in the house was five years old. Otherwise we could have figured out the right day, give or take a week. She bustled around for days before, singing bits of carols, cleaning the already clean house.

On Nancy's Christmas, she presented me with a pair of socks she'd knitted herself, one larger than the other by half.

I felt like a real shit until I remembered the Dickinson book I had squirreled away in my room. I think she believed my story about saving it for her. She asked me to read to her from it, and even snuggled up to me on the ancient sofa.

Of course, I first chose the poem that began, "Wild nights, wild nights." Nancy loved it. She walked around for days reciting several of the verses.

One night, snuggled together on the couch, the old fireplace throwing off more light than heat, I leaned over and kissed her, almost chastely, on the forehead. I felt content and complete. I would gladly have spent the rest of my life in that place, with that woman.

Nancy looked at me with an unreadable expression on her face, an expression I hadn't seen before — and I thought I'd seen them all.

She didn't move away, not an inch, but said, "I'm sorry, Vic, I really am, but I can't do what you want. I know what you want. I almost understand. But I was raised to believe it's wrong. Very wrong. And now, even though I have strong feelings for you, well, they're not that kind of feelings. I just can't do that."

I was astounded, even shocked. I could only mumble, "What are you talking about?"

"I know what you are, Vic. I think I knew from the start. I didn't think it would be a problem, but now I'm afraid it's getting to be. I don't want you to think about me like that anymore."

"Nancy, I can't help what I think, how I feel."

"Maybe not entirely, but you can force yourself to think of other things. And you can stop watching me bathe, and we could move further apart. I could take the room at the end of the hall."

"I've never tried to force myself on you, have I?"

"No."

"And I wouldn't. Not ever. I'm willing to wait for you. I love you, Nancy."

"And I love you, Vic. Just not in the same way. I could never do what you want, be what you are."

"What I am? What I am is a woman who loves women. That doesn't make me less female, or less human, or less anything. I don't know what you've been told, what you believe, but we've lived together this long. Do I have horns? Am I a devil? Nancy, look at me! I love you. I'm in love with you. I want you. But I'm not going to force you. I want to touch you so bad my fingers ache, but I want you to want me, too. I want you to come to me. I'll play the game your way. You sleep in any room you want. You bathe in private. But you can't tell me how to look at you, how to feel. You can't tell me not to love you. And I'll wait. And I'll wait as long as it takes. Just promise me one thing. Please. If you ever change your mind, let me know. Come to me. Please."

Nancy just sat there. She did not move away. We sat in silence for a long time.

Finally she said, "There's something I have to know."

"Okay."

"That day you went to town and stayed so late and came home without anything but knitting needles and yarn?"

I knew what was coming. I just knew.

"You met someone in town, didn't you?"

I looked at her and knew she expected the truth, but that she wouldn't like it. "Yes, Nancy, I did."

"A woman?"

"Yes."

"Like you?"

"You mean a demon?"

"No, Vic, a . . . a . . ."

"Lesbian. The word is lesbian."

Nancy winced and looked quickly away. After another silence, she asked, "Did you?"

"Did I? Make love? Have sex? *Do it?* Yes, yes, yes!"

Nancy looked at me as if I were something nasty. Something even worse than a dyke. "How could you?"

"It was pretty easy, actually."

"That's not what I mean. You said you love me. How can you say you love me and you'll wait for me and still . . ." Her eyes brimmed with tears.

In less than an hour she'd gone from telling me to leave her alone to acting like I'd cheated on her. Before I could think, I was holding her face in my hands, my face mere inches away.

"Come to bed with me, Nancy. Come with me, and I'll never be with anyone else again. I swear it!"

Her tears were hot on my hands, scalding.

Seven seconds is a very long time to wait for an answer to a request like that. Seven seconds felt like the total length of eternity.

Nancy shook her head no, over and over. Then she pulled away from me. "It's wrong, Vic. It's terrible and disgusting." She turned and ran up the stairs to her room. The slamming of the door was a physical injury.

I licked Nancy's tears off my hands.

CHAPTER 9

It occurred to me during my first trip back to town that since the winter had been so mild, I probably hadn't needed to wait so long. Nancy and I had psyched ourselves into equating winter without snowplows with winter imprisoned. I tucked Nancy's shopping list into the visor and drove straight to Bertha/Jane's.

She greeted me with a bone crushing hug.

"Damnit, woman, you sure kept me waiting. I thought I told you to hurry back!"

"Winter," I mumbled, my only excuse.

"Winter, shit," she said, "you coulda made it in, easy. You get your little friend to come through for you?" The words sounded like an accusation, but she was laughing. "You probably don't need me anymore."

"Let me show you how much I need you," I said, unhooking her overalls and leering. We didn't even make it to her bed.

Later we lay in each other's arms. She was so much easier to talk to than Nancy. I never felt I had to be strong or put on any false fronts with Bertha. We talked about the town.

"You said you'd always lived here," I said. "Isn't it hard to see it this way?"

Bertha took a deep breath before she answered. "Kinda. I never really fit in, but we sort of accepted one another. After Hank died, and Ruthann and I took up together, we were sort of the village freaks. I didn't much care, it never got vicious, just snide, if you know what I mean. Once in a while I'd sort of wish their collective clits would fall off, but I never wished anything like this on 'em."

"You must have had some friends."

"A couple. Nobody real close. Ruthann, of course. Funny thing is, I really miss the Baptist preacher's wife. She was always real nice to me, even though she must've known what I was. Most churchy folks were the meanest. 'Cept her."

"Others? Did others make it?"

"A few, all women. No men. No kids. No old folks."

"How do you live? I mean, is there a well? I'm sure you have a longstanding credit account at the grocery store."

"Yes and no." She chuckled. "Well, at first we drank up the distilled water and water in water heaters. Damned if I hadn't forgot the hand pump at the village park. There was talk, about ten years ago, of replacing it with a regular fountain, but they never quite got around to it. Then there's canned juices, pop, beer. I've developed a real taste for warm beer. How 'bout you?"

"No, thanks. Icy cold or not at all."

"No, I mean how are you getting on?"

"Hand pump. We're living in a farmhouse west of town about twelve mlles. Buried the old guy who lived there."

"Gibson place?"

"Yeah, you know it?"

"Sure do. Maybe I'll get out to visit you one of these days."

"Great. I wish you would. Better still, why don't you come live with us? Plenty of room. Plenty of water. We even take baths, Bertha/Jane."

"I do the best I can, thank you very much for the hint. And what's with the Bertha/Jane shit? I told you, I want to be called Jane. Just Jane, damnit!"

But again, her words were angrier than she was. I began to wonder if she ever really got mad.

"Sorry, babe. I always think of you as Bertha-slash-Jane. You know, as in, and/or. Bertha's too homely, and Jane, well, you're just not a Jane either. How about BJ?"

"BJ. Sounds obscene. But okay, it's BJ. Guess you could call me anything you want." She moaned as I began to knead her fleshy bulk. Her body was like bread dough set to rise. I knew what she would smell like baking.

After another round of lovemaking, I asked again, "What about it?"

"Let me catch my breath, for God's sake!" She panted, grinning wolfishly.

"Dumb shit. I didn't mean that. I meant come out to live with us."

"I don't know. I still got work to do. Let me think on it."

"What work?"

"The town. I take care of it," she explained. "I take out the garbage."

My expression must have asked the rest of my questions.

BJ went on. "Didn't you notice anything missing?" she asked. "Like, bad meat, imported and domestic? I hauled it off."

"How? To where?" I was fascinated.

"By wheelbarrow and W.W. Two gas mask. To McIntyre's swimming pool."

"Wait, wait." I was confused. "You buried the town in a swimming pool?"

"Well, it wasn't finished, but it would've been a swimming pool. In-ground. Olympic-sized. McIntyres always had to have bigger and better than anyone else. I made sure they were the first in their own pool. They would have wanted it that way." BJ chuckled, and went on. "I spent what seemed like forever hauling our fine citizens to McIntyre's back yard, one by one. One helluva pool party. Then I dumped a couple shovelfuls of lime on each one to keep the smell down. I cleared all the bad meat from the stores and threw that in too."

Something in me that I would never have recognized made me ask, "They're all there? You can see them?" Something horrible in me wanted to know.

But BJ's pragmatism saved me from my own grisly curiosity. "Hell no. Construction crew left their backhoe. It don't take no genius to figure how to use a backhoe. Covered them up real good. Heaped up the dirt to allow for settling."

"There was room for everybody?"

"Every body." BJ chuckled again.

I knew she would be a real asset on the farm. She was strong, persistent, practical, and good-humored. But I began to wonder if she was completely sane. I would not have had the stomach for what she had done.

I told her so.

"Hell," she said, "it wasn't pretty. It wasn't fun either. But now it's done. Now I got other projects."

"Like?"

"Well, I'm figuring on getting all the cars in town and parking them in all the parking lots and leaving them there with their keys in 'em. Then, if someone comes along and wants one, they can just leave one, take one. I'm working on sinking a hand pump into the holding tank at the gas station. And I was thinking of emptying all the houses of their canned goods, toilet paper, manual can openers, that sort of thing. Make them available for everyone."

"You're going to do this all by yourself?"

"Why not? Unless I can enlist these zombies.

They're mostly just waiting to die. Can't see no possibilities, you know? Can't see no future."

"How many are there?"

"Three, plus me."

I began calculating the possible ratio of survivors, if it was national, or even global. How many might have made it. The village boasted 11,500. Four were left. One in 2,875 lived. Our state had had something like 9,260,000 people: 3,091 left? Could that be right? The nation had maybe 250,000,000. The calculations took a long time and made me sick. Possibly 87,000. Good God, how could that happen?

"What was the population of the world, BJ?"

"I don't know. I know what you're doing, Vic. I'd advise you to stop. It's too damn depressing."

She was right, the figures were too damn depressing. I fell into a fitful sleep. It was dark when I woke.

BJ opened cans of smoked oysters and asparagus. We drank warm beer and held each other for hours.

I didn't even think about Nancy or going home until it was too late. I guess I didn't want to. With Bertha, I could just be the screaming dyke I was.

We slept well in BJ's messy bed.

Like a shamefaced teenager, rebellious the night before, drunk on illicit love and warm beer, I slunk home in the morning, armed against indignation and accusation with a prepackaged apology and gifts. I expected either total fury or total silence.

Nancy ran out of the garage and down the driveway to meet me. She ran up beside the car jabbering and pointing. She was almost hysterical. I could only understand, "Hurry, Vic, hurry."

I ran with her to the garage door. She was already kneeling on the dirt floor pointing to one straw-strewn corner.

Broken, empty eggshells lay in the straw. Several yellow puffballs bobbed around the floor. Nancy was crying, sobbing into her hands. I knelt beside her, clumsily putting an arm around her shoulders.

"Vic," she sobbed. "Vic, they're babies. They're babies, Vic."

I wiped her tears away, confused. "Yes, but isn't that good?"

"Yes, oh yes," she breathed. That frightening inner light shone brilliantly behind her eyes. "Yes, yes, yes, it's good. It's wonderful. Babies. Aren't they beautiful? Oh God, they're beautiful."

By the end of the week, Nancy had dozens of baby chicks to care for and to love. The light in her eyes was breathtaking. She was euphoric. She chattered and laughed and talked to the chicks, holding them to her face, even kissing them.

It was incredible to me that she didn't even seem to notice how wrong they were. A few were fine, but most were just wrong. In horrible ways. One had webbed feet, one had a thick beak, one had double wings, one actually had only one leg, in the middle, with a double foot at the end of it. It hopped grotesquely.

All she saw was their beauty, their life. All I could think of were the dozens of eggs we had eaten that would have hatched into these monstrosities.

CHAPTER 10

My mother used to sit at the table in her ultra-modern kitchen waiting for her twenty-minute complete microwave meal to cook. She would thumb through one of several country magazines and dream of living simply. She sent for innumerable brochures from country inns and bed-and-breakfasts. She'd plan vacations in "enchanting rural settings" with "rustic charm" and "authentic simplicity." I guess the artificial simplicity of her own life was not enough.

Dad and I would make great shows of revulsion,

offering to turn off the electricity so she could rough it at home.

I doubt that she would have found my new lifestyle charming for long. I'd discovered the reason the old man had used his outhouse; the basic plumbing was in complete disrepair. We'd been lucky to get those first showers. Peeing in a coffee can kept under the bed loses its allure eventually. Knowing how to dig a new outhouse is one thing, but doing it is another, as is turning over a garden by hand, washing clothes in a washtub, and hauling water by the bucketful.

Nancy's garden veggies did well, nothing weird grew, at least. She started reading up on how to can, increasing the amount of vinegar, salt and sugar on the grocery run.

I started wondering how far the nearest food wholesaler was, against the day the shelves would be empty.

I also increased the frequency of my visits to town; sunshine on my shoulder makes me horny.

BJ's instant-credit car lots materialized and she started the foraging project, gathering non-perishables in a grocery cart and wheeling them back to the grocery store.

I caught her in this bizarre reverse-action on one trip in.

She waved merrily and I went straight to her house, thinking to surprise her by stripping down and waiting for her in bed. But she took longer than I calculated, so I started cleaning her messy house. That too took longer than I'd thought, so I was almost done when I heard her heavy tread on the porch. I jumped quickly into the now-made bed, thinking how pleased Nancy would have been if it had been our house I'd cleaned. But BJ just clambered in with me, laughing, not even looking.

"Don't you notice anything?" I couldn't keep up my waiting patiently for recognition game very long.

"Sure do, you lost weight. Hell, you ain't hardly got no tits no more."

"Damnit, BJ, I mean the house. I straightened your house for you."

"Hell, I know that! I was watchin' through the window."

"You were watching? Watching me clean house? Why didn't you say anything?"

"Shit, I thought it was a private thing, a fetish, cleaning naked. I figured it turned you on."

"So you just watched?"

"Hell, yes! Watching turned me on!" BJ laughed.

We'd gotten into the habit, after sex, of lying in bed, drinking warm beer and debating what had happened and what was going to happen. We worked on one theory at a time, sensing we had plenty of time, and that the answers might never come. BJ suggested theories; I debunked them.

"Nuclear war." She pronounced it "nuculer."

"No warning, no noise, no flash, no radiation sickness," I countered.

"Your friend's chickens are all messed up."

"Not all."

"Most."

"Some."

"Nuclear accident, a spill."

"The big *oops*? Nope. Too widespread, too quick. No warning, no sickness."

"Some sickness," she said knowingly.

"Minor nausea. Not everyone."

"Maybe everyone who died. You ask them?"

"Did you set sick?"

"Nope."

"Me either, but Nancy did."

"Chemical? Germ warfare? Cosmic?"

"Cosmic?" I asked.

"Yeah, like UFO dust or something?"

"Doesn't sound likely."

"You think a dead world sounds likely?" BJ could be startlingly insightful at times.

As to the future, there didn't seem to be as many possibilities. "How long you figure we can go on like this, Vic?"

"Well, Nancy's garden looks good, if we expand it next year, we might be able to start living off the land. With help, we could for sure. Nancy's not real muscular," I added pointedly.

BJ ignored my hint, as she had every other time I tried to recruit her for the farm.

"One of the zombies helped me gather food last week. If the survivors started working together, maybe there's hope. Power plants would be the best place to start, I reckon. Get electricity on again, there's no tellin'. How much you know about how power plants work?"

"Absolutely nothing. Anyway, gas lines, plumbing, would be simpler. Power plants were probably run by computers, which need ..."

"Right, electricity. Which brings us back to start."

"You think they got manuals at power plants? Like *How to Make This Baby Work If We're Not Here to Show You*."

"I doubt it, BJ, I doubt it very much. Nobody thought there'd be anybody left, did they?"

"How about a plague?"

"Too fast, it was all over in just six hours or so."

"Spores, blown on the wind?"

"From where?"

"Fungus. Toadstools on God's brain."

CHAPTER 11

BJ did come out to visit us that summer. She just pulled up one afternoon in a dark blue pickup truck loaded with one of each item left on the grocery store shelves, plus a couple bottles of gas and several bags of lime.

BJ and I started unloading the truck, swapping smart-mouth remarks. I'd forgotten that Nancy and BJ had never met, although I often talked to BJ about Nancy, and tried to talk to Nancy about BJ.

BJ was interested; Nancy was not.

"Vic." Nancy stood apart from us. "Vic, don't you think you should introduce us?"

"Hell, ma'am, I'm Ber — I mean Jane, Vic calls me BJ. I've sure heard plenty about you. Glad to meet ya."

BJ stuck out her beefy hand; Nancy's must have seemed like a child's in comparison. But at least she did shake hands with BJ. For a second, I was afraid she wouldn't.

Thankfully, Nancy was never the kind of person to be unfriendly to anyone, and BJ stole her heart about ten seconds later.

"Brought you a present," she boomed, thrusting a large bag into Nancy's arms. "Thought you might like these."

"These" were three sets of printed sheets and pillowcases, femme as hell. Eyelet lace, flowers, pinks and greens.

Nancy hugged them instead of BJ, but it might have been a toss-up. Her eyes were all teary.

Damn, I wish I'd thought of that.

BJ stayed two weeks exactly. Her profanities, obscenities and vulgarities grated on Nancy almost more than the fact that she shared my bed in spite of the availability of spare rooms.

Until well past noon every day, Nancy kept her eyes down and her back rigid, wincing at BJ's colorful speech. But BJ worked so hard at winning Nancy, trying to coax a laugh, anticipating her wants and trying to please her in dozens of thoughtful ways, that by nightfall Nancy was smiling and joking back.

Then, at night, BJ would moan with pleasure so

loud I could almost feel Nancy, on the other side of the wall, tense up.

I suggested we change rooms, maybe taking the attic. I had visions of BJ and me living up there for good. It was huge and intriguing, with the ceiling cut into by the many gables. I loved to read up there, lying on an old mattress that smelled of dust and ancient cotton.

We tried it for a while, but the tension continued to build. BJ was openly sexual, grabbing at me anytime she felt like it; Nancy acted like her legs didn't part. BJ was incorrigibly messy; Nancy was compulsively neat. BJ was large and loud and vulgar; Nancy wouldn't have said "fuck" if she had a mouthful of it. I didn't expect it to last as long as it did.

Nancy never said anything to BJ about her choice of words, but reprimanded me louder and oftener than usual, and for less. BJ started taking long walks, telling me about an apple orchard just a couple miles away, and offering to come back in the fall to see what we could harvest.

She helped me fell an old tree across the road, a hell of a grueling job. She promised to bring back a chainsaw and a can of gas, to cut it up.

After plenty of advance warning, she crawled into bed one night and said, "I'll be going back in the morning. It's time."

"I wish you wouldn't." I was disappointed if not surprised.

"This has been fun, and I'll be back now and again, but I sure as shit cannot live like this."

66

I thought of Nancy's unspoken disapproval, her eloquent silences. I asked, "Is it Nance?"

BJ wrapped her arms around me, holding tight. She nodded her head, then muttered, "I'm sorry, I really am, but now I understand."

Confused, I said, "Understand? Understand what?"

"Why you love her, even with me. Why you stay out here with her."

I didn't know what to say and stayed quiet.

Then BJ buried her face in my shoulder and mumbled, "Hell, I can't hardly keep my own damn hands off her."

BJ visited often after that, sometimes staying overnight, seldom longer. Each time she came, she brought Nancy a gift, things I should have thought of, but didn't.

Once it was house paint, thirty-seven gallons of it, five different shades of white, and dark green for the trim. Nancy had casually mentioned that the house would seem more homey if it was painted, so BJ hauled out all this damn paint, promising to do the whole thing herself. Of course, I couldn't let her get away with that, so I started painting the next morning.

Even with both of us working, it took nearly three weeks. The wood was so thirsty it just sucked up the first two coats like a chocolate shake in August. Oh my God, ice cream, I'd almost forgotten.

After it was finally finished we remembered primer. Nancy made us keep all the paint of one shade (she called it a "dye lot") on one side of the house, so the differences wouldn't be so noticeable. To whom? What could it matter in a life like this if the house were painted at all? White with green trim. At least it was latex.

I swore that if BJ promised a new roof I would throw her off of one. A tall, steep one. Ours.

We were still lovers, but somehow rivals too.

I thought she'd won when I came out of the outhouse one day to find BJ's truck in the drive and Nancy in BJ's arms. Something inside of me fell into the region of my pelvis, but to this day I couldn't tell you which one of those two I thought I'd lost.

Then Nancy was calling to me. "Vic, Vic, come see what BJ brought!"

There in the back of the truck, tethered to the tailgate, was a pair of young goats.

"Twins," BJ said, "one of each. Damned if I know where their mommy is, couldn't find her. I'll bring her out if I do."

Nancy had climbed in the truck and was making friends with the weird-eyed creatures. BJ was rocking back and forth, pleased with herself. I shook my head and walked away.

It was just too damned much. House paint and goats. BJ and Nancy.

We didn't see much of BJ over the next winter. It was colder, with more snow. The woodpile the former owner left was nearly gone and the new wood was too green. I'd started looking at the old barn in a new way when an early thaw hit, or rather, slid in. Brown earth did a slow striptease under the sun's direction, but the sweet budding promise of spring, symbol of ever-renewing life, just pissed me off royally.

Nancy's incessant optimism irritated like a canker. Even the thought of a run in to see BJ didn't interest me.

After almost two years, I was homesick. I wanted my family, my job, the kids. Martha, especially Martha.

I thought almost constantly of going back, of trying to see if she'd returned from England. I became convinced that she too had survived, that she was existing somehow in the city and was waiting for me there. I dreamed of bringing her back here, fantasized of making long slow love to her. Except in my dreams she had no face. I could almost hear her voice but I'd forgotten her face. I invented one for her, a BJ/Nancy composite which was ludicrous.

Something was born inside me that spring, something malcontented, dissatisfied and callous, frightening and powerful. Something cold.

There was no joy in my spring reunion with BJ. The physical pleasure was there, but muted, detached, as if it were happening to someone else, and I only watched.

I barely listened as BJ rambled on about a great surprise for Nancy.

"One helluva giftie," she said.

She swore me to secrecy, no sacrifice on my part. I hadn't been paying much attention, making love to Martha in BJ's body.

I thought it might be time to move on, and began plotting my escape.

Several weeks later, BJ pulled up in another pickup truck, this one with a cap on the back.

Nancy was glad to see her, though not to the degree that BJ was to see Nancy.

Nance kept looking at the truck, like a kid trained by indulgent parents to ask, What did you bring me? Of course she never said that, but she might as well have.

BJ said, "I brought you something, babydoll."

Babydoll, for Christ's sake. I swear to God she said babydoll.

"Cover your eyes, go on now. You too, Vic, cover your eyes." BJ squirmed with anticipation.

I covered my eyes, playing the game, but I didn't give a damn what BJ was up to. Mentally, I was packed already, hoped they would be happy together, glad that Nancy would not be alone when I left.

"OK," BJ said, after some scuffling and door shutting. "You can open your eyes now."

Slow motion, for eternity. Past and future and present fused by a deadening inevitability. None of us spoke, or moved, or even blinked. We stood, a tableau, posed for dramatic effect, waiting.

BJ finally spoke. "Well, what do you think? Thought they were extinct, didn't ya?"

Neither of us spoke, so BJ spoke again. "It's a man. I want you to meet Rich. Rich, this is Nancy, the one I told you about, and this is Vic. Whaddaya think? I told ya she was a looker, eh?"

He was tall, dark hair curling around and on his face. Heavy-featured, with full lips. With his thumbs hooked into his jeans pockets, his eyes were alert, calculating. He seemed to be assessing not just Nancy, but all three of us.

"Hello there," he smiled, looking expectantly into Nancy's eyes, waiting.

Nancy blushed deeply, glancing away, first at BJ, then at me, then at the ground.

I think she realized long before I did the purpose of BJ's gift. It was the expression on BJ's face that finally tipped me off.

We stood in awkward silence for an unbelievably long time. Again it was BJ who did the talking.

"Well, what say we go on in and have a beer? I brought some along, to celebrate."

The three of them went in, and I stood watching after them. It finally sunk in that BJ'd brought Nancy the only thing she really wanted. BJ gave her the one thing I never could have — a walking, talking sperm bank.

Hope for a future generation.

I damned BJ wholeheartedly and went back to turning over the garden, sodden shovelful by sodden shovelful.

CHAPTER 12

Rich was a self-satisfied, surly, selfish son-of-a-bitch, and he made no pretense of being anything else.

His existence enraged me, but Nancy's reaction to him was disgusting. She simpered and blushed and giggled at his asinine jokes. I wanted desperately to strangle her, or him, or both. She scurried here and there, attempting to please him.

I think BJ was disappointed that they didn't

mate right there in the kitchen so she could see that it was done properly.

Rich didn't seem the least embarrassed by his role as stud. I soon realized that he relished it, taking full advantage of his position as genetic material.

You understand I have never had any particular affection for the male of the species, any species, although I appreciate their role, reproductively speaking. Hey, just to show you how liberal I can be, I'll tell you I even considered artificial insemination one summer a lifetime ago. I thought I wanted a child of my own, female, of course. And I have always bought the Catholics' immaculate conception thing. I was just pissed that we all couldn't do what Mary did.

So, I might have been prejudiced against Rich from the beginning, for the simple sin of manhood. Also, maybe I was jealous of Nancy's attentions to him. This is also possible. Or maybe he simply personified every undesirable male trait. He was domineering, arrogant, self-centered and, of course, believed the axis the world spun on was his penis. He even offered it to me.

"Mine's the best. Got to be. That's why I was spared. Best cock in town, maybe the world. Might even be the only, who knows?"

Nancy blushed.

BJ chuckled.

I pictured him castrated by the jagged blade of a torn beer can.

"Satisfaction guaranteed. I got ten bellies to my credit already."

73

"Ten?" BJ seemed fascinated. "Where?"

"All over. Well, here and there. There's all these little towns run by zombies. They love me. I just keep movin' in and movin' on."

"A regular Johnny-fucking-Appleseed, aren't you?" I couldn't resist some kind of cut.

But Rich took it as a compliment. "Yeah, that's right. Johnny Appleseed. I like that!" He went on, "So, who's on first? How about you, Vic, you look like you need a real man."

"Where are we going to find one?" I sneered.

"Why, right here, little lady." He patted his crotch possessively.

"No thanks," I said, "I'd rather sew it shut."

"Vic! How vulgar!" It was Nancy, of course.

"He started it!" Instant seven-year-old.

"He *is* our guest!"

"He *is* an asshole."

But Nancy's eyes had taken on that weird translucence, and I sure as hell knew what that meant. I expected her to send me to my room, but she busied herself getting him another warm beer.

BJ came over to me and put an arm around my shoulders. She combed my hair back with her fingers, then turned my face to hers.

"Look," she whispered, trying to massage the scowl lines from between my eyes with her thumb. "He ain't much, mama, but he's all she's got. Can you give her a baby? Can I? So just shut up, OK?"

Rich caught the actions, if not the words. "Oh, I get it now. You two do each other, right? Hey, that's cool. Maybe I could watch."

"Maybe you could shit on yourself, too," I snarled as I strode out of the room.

I went back to town with BJ, at her insistence. BJ went out to the farm once a week, finally returning with the joyous news. Rich was moving on. The deed was done.

I went home.

That first pregnancy was the worst. Nancy's body seemed to take what little flesh she had to form the mound which grew steadily.

I believed she was going to die. Dark circles deepened under her eyes. She grew weaker, smiled seldom. But the light behind her eyes never went out, even when she spoke of death. She spoke often of death ...

"Under the lilacs, Vic," she would say. "If anything happens, put me under the lilacs."

I tried to joke. "The ones in the front yard or the ones by the outhouse?"

She didn't smile. "Don't stay here alone, Vic. Go stay with BJ." And another time: "Vickie." She had never called me that before, ever. "If my baby lives, will you take care of him?"

"Him! It's a him? What makes you think it's not a her?"

"Promise me. Promise me, Vic."

Nancy let me touch her a lot during this time. But there was no thrill in it for me. As I stroked her temples or kneaded her aching back or rocked her in my arms, I was terribly aware of how fragile her life was, by what a fine thread we clung.

BJ promised to come out to stay when it was about time.

"Shit! I've delivered just about every kind of farm animal you can name. Baby humans ain't so different. Mostly you just catch, clip and tie. This'll be fun."

But Nance was only six months along when I found her doubled up on her bed. She was crying and clutching her belly, and bleeding.

Oh God, so much blood.

"It's too early, he won't live. Vic, Vic, pray for me!" She sobbed.

And if prayer is a scream for help from every layer of one's being, physical and spiritual, emotional and mental, if it feels like all of your skin has been peeled off and kosher salt poured on, if it means willing an unseen and unconsidered power to acknowledge your pain, or fear, then you bet your ass I prayed. And for that brief moment Nancy and God and I were one; I felt it. Our spirits touched in agony as they never have in joy. Not yet, at least.

And as I clumsily sopped up the mingled salts of tears and blood and waters and sweat, I wished it were my own blood, or that bastard man's, or BJ's. Anyone's but Nancy's.

It seemed to take so long, eternities laid end to end, but I suppose it lasted only an hour or so. Nancy's baby was suddenly just there on the bed, oozed out with more blood. Another groan, another shudder, and the afterbirth joined the mess on the bed. I wadded it all up and buried it immediately under the lilacs, the ones by the outhouse.

I lied easily to Nancy, "It was a boy. It was born dead. Nancy, I'm so sorry."

It was a lie on all three counts. I never noticed its sex, if it had one.

As I'd carried the bundle outside, I felt one of its heads move.

I was not sorry.

Nancy's milk was present even though there was no infant to feed. Her breasts were painfully swollen and her soul seemed to have been buried in the same shallow grave as her child.

I did grieve for her loss, but that cold creature which came to live around my heart lusted thirstily for the taste of Nancy's milk. But enough of my basically decent old self survived to shame me for my bizarre fantasies and make me turn away when Nancy caught me staring at her damp, clinging shirt front.

"It hurts, Vic," she sobbed one night as we sat across bowls of tomato soup and jars of canned fruit.

I avoided her tear-streaked face, muttering, "I think it will just pass eventually."

The old man's attic library didn't include any info on unnecessary lactation or cracked nipples, and my mother believed in bottles. I could've gone to the library in town, but Nancy needed me to stay with her.

"Help me, Vic! Do something!" Still sobbing, Nancy walked around to my side of the table.

She was unbuttoning her blouse. Realizing this, I stared fixedly at my soup, as if to count the pepper particles floating there.

Then she stood beside me, trying to control her sobs, a swollen breast in each hand. They looked like overripe fruits, pomegranates, about to split their skins. She was so close to me I could see their hard heaviness as she lifted them away from her. The right one squirted thin bluish liquid across my face.

Without thinking, I brushed the milk off my face and into my mouth. I looked into Nancy's anguished eyes and read the plea. Not really believing it was happening, I took her nipples one by one into my mouth and eased her pain.

I never finished my soup.

Nancy began sleeping with me that night. She let me stroke her any way I wanted, which was limited by the postpartum blood flow, but she would not touch me. She didn't mind how much I touched myself, though, which I did, plenty.

Each night she offered full aching breasts to me to be sucked empty as I manipulated myself through orgasm after orgasm, pretending it was her hand on me.

Then we slept, my arms around her, my face in her hair.

I suppose we kept each other sane.

Belatedly bringing armloads of books on infant care and techniques of breast-feeding, BJ showed up around the time Nancy should have been due, but she didn't even stay the night when she heard the edited version of what happened. I don't know if she was driven off by the discomfort of Nancy's grief or if she sensed there was something going on between us. At any rate, she left with a promise to return in real spring.

Nancy stopped bleeding and I tried to drink less of her milk so she could dry up, but it was damn hard to do. I think I was addicted. Besides, I didn't want Nancy to return to her own room.

She allowed me to touch her in many ways except with my mouth. If she ever got off, she never showed it.

Can you fake not having an orgasm? I doubt it.

Still, she would not touch me, and her gaze was distant, but I was prepared to be patient. I believed that once I had brought her to orgasm, she would become my lover, instead of just being passive. I already knew how she tasted; I sampled her juices from my hands.

I planned to take her with my lips and teeth and tongue while she slept. Then, I thought, she would love me back.

Maybe she would have, too, except for the return of Rick the Prick. Cocky and horny, he strutted into the kitchen one morning expecting to be fed and laid. Nancy left my bed then, eyes alight.

She has never returned.

CHAPTER 13

Afraid I would murder Rich, or Nancy, or both, I left them to their nightly procedures and went to live with BJ, who welcomed me, and was happy to touch me.

"I sure as hell am glad to see you so hungry," BJ chortled after our mutual ravishment. "I was afraid I'd lost you for good." Her voice was jocular, but she eyed me speculatively.

"Just eat me, bitch," was my laughing reply. I would never tell her about Nancy and me.

She had done an astounding thing over the

winter. She had scouted other communities, discovering survivors and bringing them back to live in "BJ City" as I'd renamed her town. She brought them in, settled them down, and began organizing them and the zombies who were starting to act more like human beings, but were only too glad to let BJ lead them.

There were pitifully few of them, all women. One was pregnant. "By our old pal Rich," BJ confided. "Mr. Busy Balls himself."

"Did you warn her?" I asked, "Did you tell her about Nancy's . . . offspring?" I almost said "thing."

"Nope. No point in it. That'd only scare her worse than she is now, and that's plenty, what with no doctors handy."

"When is she due?"

"Not for quite a while yet, five or six months. Plenty of time to get her to trust me. Hell, she came here, didn't she?"

"What are you doing with them?" I asked.

"Puttin' them to work," she answered, shifting heavily in bed. "We need to start growing our own food. The canned stuff won't last forever. I might commandeer a semi and head into the big city for more, but if the survival rate's consistent, the city survivors might not appreciate that. We got enough wheat and soybeans to at least get a start. Maybe in the city we can trade fresh-grown stuff for canned."

"What if they aren't as well organized as us, I mean, you?"

"Well, maybe I'll just stay there a while and get 'em organized. Figure out what's most important, what's possible. Get things rollin', you know?"

There were bright, excited flushes on BJ's cheeks.

A powerful emotion rolled through me; I hugged her and said, "God, BJ, I love you!"

I stayed with BJ at least a month after the walking sperm-bag stopped by on his way out to tell us of "his" success at the farm. He was off to Detroit, his home base.

It was appalling to me that BJ could sit across her littered table and converse calmly with the enemy of my soul.

His "usefulness" was her defense. "He tells me stuff I need to know," she told me. "Like how many people survived, and where. How many babies we can expect. Besides, what will our needs be in a year? Five? Ten?"

"I didn't hear him say all that."

"Not in so many words, no. But he tells me what I need to know to figure it out for myself."

"He's scum," I spat, wishing I could have dug two graves under the lilacs, one larger and penis shaped.

"You're right, absolutely, but for now, he's useful scum, understand?" There was some warning in her voice which I heard but did not, in fact, comprehend.

I went back to the farm out of duty, spurred by the memory of Nancy's difficulty with that first ghastly pregnancy.

I went there with a rusty red pickup truck full of supplies — and a heart full of something between fear and hope. Fear that she would be as sick and weak as the last time, and hope that if she was, she would need me more.

When I pulled up the drive, she did not run to

meet me. She waved and went back to pumping water, the morning sun polishing her hair to bright copper. It almost hurt to look at it. As she carried the buckets of water toward the house, I noticed a transformation. Nancy had become an incredible beauty. In her I saw beauty and health and assurance. And something else. Determination? It was there in her voice, behind her words. Polite words, everyday words, distancing words.

"It's good to see you, Vic ... the chickens hatched while you were gone ... Don't you think we should expand the garden this year?"

But I heard another message, spoken with her shoulders and back, her head and eyes, those spirit-piercing eyes. It was a message I could not ignore.

It said I had lost.

Nancy would never be mine.

Right. So why didn't I leave then, before everything got complicated? Go live with BJ, or hit the road?

There was no single answer, no simple one. Perhaps I felt I owed Nancy something. I was also curious to see what this child would look like. Of rejection and humiliation, I'd had my share. Maybe I just loved her too deeply to leave. Maybe some part of me still refused to accept that she would never be mine.

For whatever reasons, I stayed. That one coppery morning moment forged the link between past and present, the link between will and fate, making it impossible to tell if either of us had any choices at all.

Nancy and me, BJ and even Rich seemed caught inextricably in an elaborate dance routine, less elegant than ballet, less intense than jazz, more like a jivy tap routine with metal plates nailed to our shoes, artificial grins nailed to our faces.

Anyone watching would have seen a joyful, reflexive response to rhythm, the beat dictating the moves, feet ad-libbing in triple time. But in reality the dancers practiced prescribed steps, mentally mouthing, *hop-shuffle-step-flap-flap-shuffle ball change-shuffle ball change . . .*

Nancy's second pregnancy proceeded more smoothly than that first one. Instead of the profound weariness and constant nausea, there was health and the legendary beauty of pregnant women. Her increasing confidence and joy made me miserable.

If the seeds, so to speak, of hope lie ever dormant in the dyke breast, I was beginning to doubt the existence of spring. As the realization of her maternal aspirations reared, her need for me decreased proportionately. If this offspring survived (I was still hesitant to use the word *child*), I would become obsolete for Nancy. As it was, I was already down to being gardener and stuck-jar-lid unscrewer.

At least I had the memory of our brief, doomed, milky encounters, which naturally served as mulch for my fantasies of us together, rather than any kind of actual fulfillment.

The less Nancy needed or wanted me around, the

more I wanted to be with BJ. I was still welcome in her life and in her bed. Playing on her affection for Nancy, I tried again to persuade her to move in with us.

"She needs you, BJ. You know she always liked you best," I teased.

"Look, Vic, I wanted to ask you about her. Something's changed between you two. Did something happen?"

I avoided her knowing gray eyes and evaded the question. "Like what?"

"Oh, maybe a fight . . . or something . . ."

I don't know how much she guessed, or sensed. BJ was sometimes uncannily canny. But I sure as hell wasn't about to tell her that her darling Nancy fell off her pedestal into Big Bad Vic's bed — especially while I was still busy in BJ's.

"Well, you know," I covered, "losing that baby really messed her up. Maybe she blames me, or something."

I also didn't want BJ to know how appropriate it would be if Nancy did blame me. I continued to avoid her eyes, which wasn't that difficult, considering what I was doing at the time.

Later that night, as we lay in her rumpled bed — the least cluttered spot in her house — she tugged absent-mindedly at my nipples and began a conversation that altered our relationship and our lives.

"Vic, I want to ask you something."

I groaned and rolled out of her reach, "Oh no! Not seconds! You greedy bitch, I'm exhausted."

BJ didn't come after me, or even smile, so I curled up under her arm again. I was sure she was going to continue questioning me about Nancy, and a cold blade of fear sliced into me.

But all she said was, "You was at college, weren't you, Vic?"

"Yup," was my well-educated and relieved reply. "Why do you ask?"

"Well, I was thinking about, well, that we'd make a great team."

I slid my palm between her heavy thighs. "I thought we already were."

"Stop that, bitch," BJ shouted. "I'm trying to talk to you here, OK?"

I don't think she'd ever been mad at me before. It surprised me. "OK, OK, I'm sorry, I'm sorry."

Then she softened, blushing. "Look, I'm sorry too, I didn't mean to bark at you. I know you really just want me for my great tongue."

"You are so right!" I leered, reaching for her again.

But before we could slip into the obvious position this conversation was leading, BJ moved to the foot of the bed and sat there cross-legged like a heavy-breasted Buddha.

"Listen, Vic. First we talk, OK?"

"About college?"

"Sort of."

"OK, what about college?"

"I didn't go."

"Too late now."

"Vic . . ." BJ warned.

"Sorry. You didn't go to college, so what?"

"So I'm not as smart as you."

"I doubt that," I answered, thinking of the mass grave in the swimming pool, the leave-one-drive-one car lot, and the hand pump sunk into the gas station tank.

"Look, I've been thinking," she said. "If the rest of the world, or even just this country, was wiped out in the same ratio as us, well, we have a chance to start all over. Only this time women will be in control. We can rebuild. We can band together and start fresh. We don't have to just survive. We won't be able to for long, anyway. Even canned goods don't last forever. What you and Nancy are doing — growing your own greens, raising chickens — that's where we should start. First, we've got to see that everyone has enough food and a job to do. And then, well, we can make laws, and courts, and new ways of living. The only man we've seen is our old pal Rich, and he's perfectly happy as a traveling stud service. He sure don't want to be president, not while he can be a god. And the other women, the other survivors, they're just waiting around, hoping someone will tell them what to do and how to do it. We can do it, Vic, I know we can."

I could only stare at BJ. I thought I knew who she was and what she wanted, what she was and who she wanted. This was a totally new side to her, a scary side, and I didn't want any part of it.

"BJ, wait. Rebuild? Laws? Courts? Armies too, I suppose? No way, babe. Count me out. I say we just let things go on as they are. If any social structure — not to mention political — is going to occur, it should just evolve, just grow naturally. You're talking about instant Western civilization. Just add water and stir. It's more complicated than that. Look what it brought us so far. We all lived for decades with the near-certainty of global annihilation. We weren't even surprised when it happened, were we? Were you? We were more surprised that we survived, that anyone survived. In all of our conjectures on the exact nature of the destruction of our world, did we ever question its inevitability? Did we ever curse the hand that killed us? No. Hell, no. All we've wondered is what means were used. We wanted to know *how* it was done. Never why. Don't you see? Humanity has always fucked up and always will."

BJ said softly, "Yes, but now we're talking about women." And after a long silence, she added, "We have to try."

"Why?" I demanded, near tears. "Why?"

"Because it's possible. We have to try because I believe it's possible."

"What do you want from me?"

"I need you to help me figure out how. Where to start. I've got the dream, the vision. You've got the education. Vic, we can do it. I need you beside me."

Another silence stretched like a thin rubber band that is sure to hurt when it breaks. I broke it.

"No. I'm sorry BJ, I really am. I don't want this to come between us, but I just can't see it. I think you should just leave well enough alone. When the food runs out, someone will think to plant. Or they won't. If they starve, they starve. We're OK, aren't we? You? Me? Nancy? Why bother? Who cares?"

"I care," she said. "I care plenty. And I can't even believe you don't. I thought I knew you, Vic."

For a long moment, I felt and saw the widening gulf between us, nonexistent just an hour before.

"OK," BJ said, sounding tired and lonely. "But will you at least tell me some books to read to get started? You know, *How to Build Your Very Own World Made Simple,* real simple."

"Ah, yes," I said, grateful for the attempted conciliation in her tone, *"Utopia."*

"Well, I don't know about utopia, but I'll do my best."

"No, no. *Utopia* was an essay before it was a word or a concept, by Sir Thomas More. Too good to be true, and it wasn't, but very interesting and probably a good place to start. And you should enjoy reading about the rule of soft lead."

"What's that?"

"Lesbian rule."

"Hot damn! You mean we ain't the first?"

My BJ was back and I hated to spoil that, but I had to say, "You, gorgeous, not *we.*"

"What else? What should I read?"

I decided to change the atmosphere in the room, if not the topic. I reached for BJ's hand, pulling her back into my arms. I kissed her fully on the mouth with each added name.

"Plato . . . Aristotle . . . Machiavelli . . . Rousseau . . . Marx . . ."

"Marx? Wasn't he a commie?"

"Not like you've been taught. He was no demon, and you should read him for yourself." I went back to listing and kissing.

"de Tocqueville . . . Locke . . ."

I was surprised how easily the names came back to me. Too bad I wasn't able to retake my poli-sci final.

I waited, hoping I had finally discouraged her and wondering if other, more physically satisfying, ideas were occurring to her.

89

She grabbed a handful of my hair, the gesture forceful yet gentle. She pulled my face away from hers. A thrill of expectation tightened my nipples.

"Wait a minute," she said gruffly. She rolled onto her side, reaching to the table beside the bed for a pencil and torn sheet of paper. Hiking herself into a sitting position and bracing the paper against her thigh, she said, "OK. Now, give them to me again."

As I grinned and moved toward her, she said, "The names, Vic, the names."

CHAPTER 14

I returned to Nancy and the farm, although all we really had was a large garden, growing larger each year. As I looked over the expanse of farmland — unused but fertile, like a hopeful aging virgin — part of what BJ had tried to express became real to me. We did need some kind of organized effort beyond Nancy and me.

Of course, I didn't really think anymore about BJ's fantasy, because I didn't really think she'd want to read a dozen ancient philosophers.

Late that summer, however, BJ pulled up in yet

another pickup truck and began unloading box after box of books.

"What the hell is all this?" I didn't mind cursing when I was with her, but watched myself around Nancy.

"Books, you dumb dyke," BJ boomed. "Every damn one of them you suggested and a whole heap more." She picked a couple off the top and handed them to me.

Flipping open the cover of one, my heart lurched sickeningly as I saw what library she had made this massive withdrawal from. It was mine, I mean, from Jackson, my town, the library where I'd met Nancy. My last remembered view of home.

"You went there? This is where I lived, I didn't know you were going there."

"Yeah, well, hell, I just thought you'd like to have some mementos from home." She called them moe-mentos.

Confused, I asked, "Were there many . . . people?"

"Yes and no," said BJ. "Give me a hand getting these in the house, will ya? I'm staying the winter. Be here for Nancy — you know, when she has her kid, help out, you know. Shit!" BJ blushed with the embarrassment of having, and showing, a gentle side.

"Tell me," I said as we hoisted and carried, "about the people."

"Looks to me like it's about the same proportion of people as we've met up with so far. And they're about in the same condition. Aimless, hopeless, sorta scavenging. They seem worse off than we are. I managed to get a group of them to listen to me about coming out here, living with us in town."

Again I thought of the smelly water in Jackson, and I tried not to notice that "living with us in town" excluded Nancy and me, but maybe she counted the farm as town, too. I remembered Martha, and a distant sadness arose. I shook it off.

BJ was still talking, more to herself than me. "It'll be more efficient that way, you know, easier to . . ."

"Control?" I offered.

"No, no. Organize, easier for them to cooperate. Showed them how to siphon gas out of the gas stations. Nobody'd thought of that. At least I don't think so. But somebody'd got ahold of a lot of something flammable."

I was about to correct her pronunciation when I noticed she was staring at me intently. "What is it, BJ? What's the matter? Why are you looking at me like that?"

She hesitated before saying, "Well, I guess you might as well know, there's a lot of your town gone. Burnt down. Looks like somebody tried to cremate the bodies, one by one. Looks like it sorta got outta hand. It's a mess, Vic, a real mess. I'm sorry."

"It's all right, BJ, I grew up in Ohio. I'd only lived in Jackson a couple years. I liked it there, but I left too, remember. With Nancy. This is our home now. I've never even thought of going back."

But something about her news made me feel sad, and a little guilty. I refused to dwell on Martha, whether she'd survived.

"I got some more news for ya, too." BJ was grinning. "Somebody else's been busy, it seems. Some of the ones coming to town are pregnant. By their descriptions I'd guess the father's our old pal Rich. I'm surprised his cock don't fall off."

"Son of a bitch!"

"Daughters, too, let's hope."

At the sound of BJ's sonic boom laugh, Nancy woke from her nap, swollen-eyed and big-bellied.

"BJ," she said, trying unsuccessfully to hug her, butting bellies. "It's so good to see you! What are you doing here? What are you laughing about?"

BJ kept her arm around Nancy, her hand resting where Nancy's waist would have been. "I'm staying 'til spring, darlin'. I'm gonna read these here books and try to get smart like Vic here, and I'm laughing 'cause I feel good. I feel real good."

"You're going to read all these books?" Nancy voiced our mutual disbelief.

I tried to explain. "BJ thinks we should try to organize whoever's left, try to rebuild. She wants to read these books to formulate a guideline."

"Oh," said Nancy. "I have the book you need." She waddled into the dining room and back, plopping the Gibson Family Bible on top of the box BJ was wrestling upstairs.

BJ shot me a quick look, then silently started upstairs again.

Nancy looked wonderingly at the boxes stacked in the kitchen, books representing several thousand years of philosophical thought. She called up to BJ, "Are you really going to read all these books?"

BJ's voice drifted down to us.

"Sure, why not? I got all winter, don't I?"

* * * * *

The first three books BJ read weren't about social structures or political ideals, but about umbilical cords and contractions. She was preparing for her new role as midwife. She and Nancy spent hours poring over pictures that sickened me. But they had not seen what I had, did not know what I knew.

BJ walked around muttering instructions to herself, like, "Don't cut the cord until the placenta is born," and Nancy rolled names around like marbles across the floors. "Sarah, Michael, Roberta, Daniel, Mark."

I tried to enter into the spirit of the thing, banished ghosts of polyhedrons.

"Look, Nance, this is a whole new world, right? So why stick to traditional names? Why not think up something new?" I tried to come up with an example. Failed. "How about Ybab?" I finally offered.

"Ybab?"

"Yeah, that's baby backwards."

"Bite your tongue."

"Or maybe Dik! Or maybe Idkay. Abybay."

BJ joined in. "Vic's right, Nancy, at least in theory. We can name her anything. Names mean something, right? Let's name it a meaning, like . . . Survival. I like that — Survival."

"Or Hope," Nancy tried.

"Epoh," was my version.

"How about No Regrets."

"Or Steven."

"Steven?" BJ and I said with a synchronized groan.

We tried again.

"Equality."

"Ichthyosaur."

"Icky for short."

"Gloria."

"Reconstruction."

"Super Glue."

"George."

"George?"

"It was my father's name," Nancy defended. "And his father's."

"George?" BJ and I groaned again, our duet perfected by practice.

Nancy, of course, was not amused. She had just tilted her chin in a gesture that preceded her I'll-have-you-know speeches. But I was learning to short-circuit her tempers. I dropped to my knees, hands in supplicant mode. With my very best voice of anguish, I knee-walked to Nancy, pleading, "Just please, please, please, Miz Nancy, if it is a girl, do not, for pity's sake, name her Victoria Louise Alicia Jane."

I only meant to placate her, but I went too far. BJ and Nancy both stared at me in silence, looking shocked. I should have just blasphemed, instead, or taken the name of defecation in vain.

As I glanced first at BJ, then at Nancy, the silence seemed interminable.

Finally BJ spoke. "Vic?"

Another silence. I didn't answer.

"Vic?"

Another.

"Oh, my God, is that your name? No. I don't believe it. Vic?"

Nancy burst into giggles.

It was my turn to be unamused.

"Say it again, Vic," Nancy said. "I want to hear it again."

"Hey, Vic, did you hear the lady? She wants to hear it again." BJ had joined forces with Nancy.

Having difficulty regaining my dignity while still on my knees, I rose slowly and, I hoped, proudly. "I was named for all four of my great aunts, each of whom was independently wealthy. My parents were not fools." The fiction had always worked on my classmates, at least until high school. But it didn't work on either BJ or Nancy.

The truth burst from BJ as if she read my mind. "You mean they couldn't make up their minds?"

"Exactly," I admitted. Exposed, I always confess. "But wait!" I commanded as the giggles began again. "This is exactly my point. Tell me, am I a Victoria Louise Alicia Jane?"

BJ and Nancy glanced at each other, forcing back their laughter with layered hands. Simultaneously, they shook their heads.

"What kind of name is that for any kid, much less a dyke? Why don't parents wait to name their kids until they find out who they are? Or at least until they get a look at them?"

This thoughtless slip brought instant regret. The only appropriate name for Nancy's firstborn would have been Hedy, assuming it was female. *Bad joke, Vic,* I chided myself.

Nancy and BJ, however, knew nothing of my faux pas, and the conversation continued.

BJ said, "Not a bad idea, didn't the native Americans do that, or something like that. Dream names for the kids, or the kids would dream names for themselves at puberty?"

"I wonder if that's where the expression came from — to 'dream up' a name?" I wondered.

Nancy said, "So what did the Indians call their kids before puberty?"

Silence.

Then BJ and Nancy, together, said, "VICTORIA LOUISE ALICIA JANE!"

CHAPTER 15

The days and weeks of that winter passed quickly, at least for me. Having BJ with us, where I could get my hands on her, cuddle near her, was what I imagined marriage to be like. I guess we were sort of married as it was. We kept separate rooms, not just for Nancy's sensibilities, but to avoid arguments about how much mess was acceptable.

BJ's room was impossible. Clothes, books, and papers lay wherever she dropped them. She never made her bed.

I usually made my bed.

Nancy always made her bed.

Which meant something, I suppose.

Of course, having separate rooms was only technical privacy. We never closed our doors, and BJ and I often slept together, usually in her bed. I went to hers more often than she came to mine. Which also probably meant something. At the time, we were just living, with no need to analyze how, no need to wonder where and how it started going wrong.

We all slipped into our roles. No one imposed them on us; no one dictated them to us. We never sat down and discussed who should do what. Nancy cooked because Nancy could cook. I burned everything I tried and BJ thought she'd cooked if she opened a can, never mind heating the contents.

I fetched and carried. BJ did repairs, like the loose basement stair. And it was BJ who sunk the hooks in opposite walls of the kitchen so Nancy could string an indoor clothesline.

We worked together, planned together; we seldom argued. We three were the perfect couple. We each had two wives. Except that Nancy absolutely shut down, cold and rigid, if either of us even joked about recruiting her to our lovestyle.

One night BJ decided it would be fun to camp out in front of the fire. We dragged my mattress down the stairs and Nancy brought armloads of quilts and pillows, but refused our invitation to stay.

"Maybe next time." She smiled indulgently, the only grown-up at the slumber party.

Close to the heat, BJ and I cuddled spoon-fashion, with me in front. Soon I felt her fingers lightly trace the line of my hip. Delicious expectation caught my breath. BJ made good love.

She sculpted my desire, an artist knowing what she wanted, how to achieve it. I was slippery with compliance. The only thing I liked as much as having her make love to me was making love to her. Every encounter seemed endless, yet done too soon.

By then, she knew every part of my body and how it reacted to what kind of touch, in what sequence, for how long, how tight, how deep. She even knew about the nape of my neck, how like a kitten, I surrendered instantly to the grasping of the hair there.

Tough, cynical Vic turned to weeping gelatin, limp and totally submissive at this gesture, and only BJ had ever discovered it. She used it to roll me onto my back, still kneading, feathering, tweaking.

A smile — half desire, half satisfaction — curled on her face. It aroused her to arouse me.

Neither her size nor my admiration for her had diminished one ounce since we'd met. I looked at her broad, capable-looking face, felt her hands, her fingers, now her thumb. Something wide and dense dropped deep inside of me. I recognized it by the feeling of helplessness that filled in the void behind its fall. I rushed to name it, to say the words, helpless and hopeful, both emotions and several more ricocheting off the sides of the well.

"BJ," I gasped, suffocating with the truth of it, clutched tightly in an orgasm of body and mind and spirit. "BJ. Oh God. I love you. I . . . love . . . you."

It was as if I had never said the words before, not to her, not to anyone. Not this way. Each word of equal weight and distance. Each word of equal value. Statement of fact. No demand for recompense. No ransom for promises to be put in a brown paper bag. No ankle chains of affection. Just the acknowledgment of my state of being.

I hunger.

"I ..."

I thirst.

"love ..."

I love.

"... you."

BJ's grin cracked open her whole face, a gleeful walnut.

"Hell, woman, I know that. Did you just figure that out? We have loved each other from the first time we made love. Shit! That ain't no surprise to me." Then she paused, examining my face as if I wore a new one. "But I got to admit," she finally said, "the words sound pretty damn good." Another pause. "I love you, too, you know, Vic. Shit! I thought you knew. I love you, too."

We left the mattress downstairs. BJ said, "Let's do that again tonight."

Nancy missed the penetrating look BJ gave me and said, "Was it warmer down here?"

BJ grinned. "Yup. A whole heap warmer." She winked at me. "Hot even."

"Maybe we should move the beds down here until spring," Nancy suggested. "I get pretty cold at night."

Stupidly, I said, "I guess you would, without anyone to sleep with."

BJ glared at me. "Hey, I've got it. Let's move

south. Why freeze at all? We could have a summer home and a winter home. Hell, we could have a different home every month."

"Then it wouldn't be home," Nancy said. "Home is where you stay. I don't want to move." But she said it softly, with a catch in her voice. She kneaded the small of her back.

BJ moved behind her, gently shoving Nancy's hands away and taking over the massage herself. Her voice was tender as she asked Nancy, "What's the matter, baby? Got the blues?"

Nancy turned and sagged into BJ's arms, sobbing. She didn't even fight for control, just let her misery and fear flow.

"Lonely," she choked. "I'm so damn lonely."

For Nancy to swear was inconceivable. That she could feel lonely, here with us, was unbelievable. I started to say something, but BJ shot me a quick look and shook her head.

Nancy clung to BJ, naming her woes between sobs. "You have each other ... to ... to hold. I can't do it. I tried ... I can't talk to you ... you don't understand how I feel ... about God ... and faith ... or anything. You think I'm stupid ... I brought us here, didn't I, didn't I? Because I listened. You don't listen ... and I can't leave ... if we move ... what if this baby dies, too? How will Rich find us? I have to keep trying ... I have to ... if my baby lives then I'll have someone ... someone to hold ... and I want my mother ... you don't bake me birthday cakes ... and I want my dog ... but she's dead, too. Everyone's dead. My baby's going to die. Oh, God, I'm so scared."

BJ picked Nancy up in her arms as if she weighed no more than an armload of firewood and carried her into the living room. She placed her on the mattress, on her side. She put a pillow folded double under Nancy's head and continued to massage her back in small, firm circles, talking softly to her. I put more wood on the fire, as much to hear what she was saying as to be helpful.

She was murmuring consoling words, words of comfort. "There, there, it's all right, I'm right here, we're both here. We care for you very much. Nothing's going to hurt you. Make some tea, ok?"

It took me a couple of beats to realize she was talking to me, since she didn't look up or change her tone. Then I saw why. BJ's face was covered with her own tears.

I moved silently to the kitchen, pouring the water kept hot all day on Nancy's wood-burner. I climbed onto the counter to reach the top shelf of the cupboard, which went all the way to the high ceiling. Nancy loved the fragile teacups stored there but said they were too good for everyday. Well, this wasn't everyday.

I balanced the cups, saucers and teapot on a tray. You wouldn't think anyone could screw up tea, would you? But it was strong as coffee, undiluted.

Nancy's sobs were down to hiccups by the time I got back. I sat at Nancy's feet. Her head was in BJ's lap. She held the pillow tightly in front of her, like a personal flotation device. Still on her side, she rocked herself gently. She stared into or beyond the fire.

BJ offered promises like bribes. "Your baby will

be just fine, you'll see. Haven't we been reading up on it? And look, about moving, you don't have to do anything you don't want to do."

As amazing as seeing BJ's tears was not hearing BJ's obscenities. They were totally absent as she reassured Nancy, who only nodded once in a while or blinked to show she was listening. She even smiled weakly when BJ promised that she would never ever, *ever* let me make tea again.

Finally, BJ said seriously, "And about Rich, if you want him to stay here, you let me know. I'll arrange that."

There was something deadly in her voice that chilled me even more than the thought of Rich here with Nancy permanently.

Nancy closed her eyes, with what I thought was wistfulness. Like BJ, I would have said anything to make Nancy happy again. I swallowed my hatred of Rich like a piece of unchewed meat and said, "Yeah, Nance, you could even get married if you want to. If you can baptize me, BJ can marry you and Rich. I always wondered why you, with your, er ... convictions, didn't insist on that before."

BJ glanced at me, amazed, probably, that I could overcome my revulsion for Rich.

"Would you like that?" she asked Nancy. "I never thought of that. Would you want to marry Rich?"

Nancy was quiet for a minute, then she giggled. "Nah, he's yucky."

Nancy slept the rest of the day away, lying on

her side, sometimes moaning in her sleep. When she moaned, BJ would go to her, kneel down, and rub her back. Sometimes Nancy would get up to go to the bathroom, then she would return to the same position.

I hadn't paid that much attention when they were studying their childbirth books, or I would have realized what was going on.

About nightfall, Nancy got up and left the room. I thought she'd just gone to pee again, but after a while, I heard rattling in the kitchen. When I went to investigate, there was Nancy, up on the counter.

"Hey, I'll put those cups away," I scolded. Then I saw she wasn't putting cups in, she was taking stuff out. She had a bucket of soapy water at her knees.

"These cupboards need a good scrubbing. Here, take these." She handed me a stack of plates.

"What the hell do you think you're doing?"

BJ came in behind me, saw what was going on and laughed. "It's ok, Vic. This is pretty normal, I think. Toward the end, I mean." Then she made a gesture to me that Nancy didn't see, a pointing down gesture, and mouthed what I read as "tonight."

"Tonight what?" I asked.

BJ rolled her eyes and shook her head. "Asshole," she mouthed.

Nancy turned to look at BJ, then at me, her blue eyes questioning. "Tonight what?" she repeated.

BJ moved to the counter and started helping her empty the shelves.

"I figure you're gonna have that kid tonight, or tomorrow, that's all."

Nancy looked at us, considering. "Well," she said,

"I'm ready if you are." Then she returned to her cupboard-cleaning.

BJ was right. Nancy went into hard labor several hours later. They worked like a team; I tried to keep out of the way. It didn't take long.

Guilty conscience and fear tortured me. Nancy had hinted at our perverse relationship earlier, but BJ didn't seem to pick up on it. Who knew what Nancy might say under this kind of pressure?

There was no doubt that either of my guilty secrets would damage, if not destroy, my relationship with BJ. I loved both women, in totally different ways. We three needed one another. Weren't we all the family we had? What if Nancy found out what I'd done to her firstborn? What if BJ found out what I did to Nancy? No! No! No! Nancy came to me. She was not seduced. She was over twenty-one. And, damn it, *she* came to *me*. BJ would have done the same thing. She would never have refused Nancy, never.

And the baby, well, they hadn't seen it. I didn't plan to kill it. I just reacted to the horror of it. Maybe I could go dig it up, show it to them. Maybe it would be possible still to see how wrong it had been, how terrible to look at. How fast did dead babies, dead animals, decompose? I think I was on my way out to the lilacs when BJ's voice broke through my terrible imaginings.

"Vic! Vic, get over here!" The urgency was in the tone, not the volume.

On my mattress on the floor, I knelt beside BJ at Nancy's open knees. I watched her baby being born. Its head came out first, its one head. Then its body. It squirmed, all slippery and shiny.

Nancy pleaded, "Keep it alive." But she wasn't talking to us.

BJ handed it to me as she occupied herself with scissors, string, towels — the cord business.

"What is it?" Nancy whispered, "Is it all right?"

I didn't answer, so BJ said, "It's a boy, Nan. You have a son."

"Oh God, please let me see him!"

"In a minute, darlin'. We want to make him pretty for you."

She wiped its face. Tiny, wrinkly face. Tiny perfect features.

Nancy laughed, "Hurry up, I want to see him. Does he have all his fingers and toes?"

I'd never told her how messed up the first one was, so it was a stock question, asked without any real concern.

I counted. "Yup, ten fingers, ten toes."

And there were. Tiny perfect appendages, complete with incredible miniature nails, transparent fragile fingernails and toenails. And the perfect little hands were connected directly onto its shoulders, and its perfect little feet were connected where the thighs would have been connected, if it had had thighs, if it had had legs at all.

BJ said to her, "Well, he's got a few problems, but the most beautiful face."

With no other warning, she handed him to her, no blanket or covering at all.

Nancy looked him over solemnly, fondling his

toes, his fingers. She held him close and kissed his perfect face about nine hundred times.

"I don't care, darling," she whispered. "Mommy loves you just the way you are."

She opened her nightgown to offer him her breast, and I left the room.

CHAPTER 16

Thankfully, Nancy was so immersed in motherhood that she didn't notice how unenchanted I was with little George.

She named him George, which was probably better than Handy Andy. Anyone would have thought that the child was edible, a precious confection, the way she constantly nuzzled him. He only cried when he needed something, like Nancy's sweet milk or the shit scraped out from between his toes. BJ had brought out several huge boxes of disposable diapers, which fit him oddly, and which

Nancy used as if they were still being manufactured. She kept the baby clean and sweet-smelling and took him to sleep in her bed. She seemed to have some kind of timer in her head, not allowing even BJ to hold him for more than thirty seconds. I know, I counted. I never asked to hold him, saving Nancy the anxiety. I didn't want to hold him. Wrapped in his blankets, with just his face showing, he looked normal, more than normal. Beautiful. But I knew that, holding him, you wouldn't be able to help noticing there was something missing. Or, rather, some things.

BJ looked at me oddly the first time I took an interest in her studies, but then she shrugged, if not understanding, at least accepting my need to get involved in something, anything that had nothing to do with our domestic life.

"Hey Beej, how about I help you with this mess?" I gestured toward her floor. "Organize, file, whatever."

"I know where everything is," she said.

"How?" I asked, amazed. Her room looked like it had been put through a blender. Pureed.

"I know where I put it," she answered. Pointing to one pile after another, she named her notes, "Religion. Justice. Agriculture. Education — that, by the way, is where you come in."

"Me?"

"You taught before."

"Yeah, but ..."

"OK, so you do again."

"No."

"What no?"

"Just no. No teaching. I'll cut wood."

"What the hell are you talking about? You *are* a teacher."

"Was. I *was* a teacher. Like you were Bertha. Now you are BJ. Now I am a gardener, a woodcutter, a chicken plucker. I kill chickens real good, don't I? I learned from scratch, pardon my pun. Whatever anyone needs to know, they can learn from scratch. Not from me."

"Vic, you have to put something back."

"Back? Put something back? I didn't take anything out."

"I thought you decided to help me."

"I did. I have. But I want to help in my own ways, not be dictated to."

"Are you calling me a dictator?"

"Well, it wouldn't take much."

"Fuck you, clitlicker, I am not a dictator. I'm just a doer. A leader, maybe."

"That's what they all said, at first."

"I am not planning on building myself a fortune. I'm not planning taxes at all. I don't want mass executions."

"You'd be a tad late."

"Listen, bitch, you can criticize when you have a better idea, not before."

"Another dictate?"

"Vic, did you come up here just to annoy me? Just to piss me off? 'Cause that's what you're doing, pissing me off."

BJ was more indignant than angry. She started

gathering papers from the floor, under and between and out of books. Scraps and sheets and tablets of paper written on sideways, crossways, in margins with her large up-and-down script. She gathered them into a messy pile, like autumn leaves, and threw them into my hands.

"Here," she said, "make yourself useful. Sort this shit out. Then we'll go over it, decide what to use and what to toss out. I just wrote down everything that seemed right to me. Now get out of my room. Please."

That was the first time BJ threw me out of her room, and the first time she shut the door.

It took me three whole days to sort BJ's notes into stacks on the floor of my room. I read each page, of quotations mostly, which concerned three or four topics at a time. I didn't see how BJ had organized her thoughts until I realized that her themes had nothing to do with any of the particular books she'd been reading. Each page of writing, every scrap, included at least one reminder to herself, and sometimes whole lists of things to be done. Useful, necessary things that no one else was thinking of. BJ was a practical, resourceful person busting her butt trying to be a theoretician. She wanted to write a new Constitution, set up a new social order, maybe be president, but she made lists. One said:

Food — find warehouse
Mark houses that have wood-burners — red paint

Talk to Nancy and Vic about warmer climate.

And she'd make it seem so offhand, a spur-of-the-moment thought. What a wily wench.

People — gather — put to work
Horses
Body fat?

What the hell was *that* about?

Later, after dinner, with her papers spread out on the dining room table and a kerosene lamp for light, she asked me, "Well, what do you think?"

Unsure how to begin, I paused before saying, "Well, you've really been working hard on this. There is a lot of good stuff here. I'm impressed with how comprehensive your initial research has been. You would have made a great researcher, BJ."

I knew I sounded like a patronizing ass, even as I said the words, which were true and what she wanted to hear, but completely beside the point.

Nancy walked in, carrying her sleeping baby. She couldn't bring herself to put him down even when he slept. She glanced at the notes I'd made. BJ's duty roster.

"What's this? 'Mark houses that have wood-burners — red paint'? What for?"

"I want to bring more people to the town. Set them up in houses that have wood-burners or fireplaces. I thought I'd start in spring, seriously scouting the villages and other small towns for people. Maybe there are more men, too. And I want to find out what they know, what they can do, put them to work. They, I mean we, can share our knowledge, teach one another, help one another. I hope to find a doctor, a welder, a mechanic. And farmers, real farmers — we need them most of all.

And we need to find out what animals survived, and bring them here, too. If there are cows we can have milk and butter and cheese again. To say nothing of beef. I want to get moving on this stuff. We've waited too long now. And horses, I'm hoping we can find horses; the gas tanks won't last forever."

"We already have goats," offered Nancy.

"I can't ride no goat."

"Not for riding, for milk and cheese. And goat is edible, too." Nancy's voice went to a kind of whisper at the last part. BJ's color was high, visible even in the dim lamplight. Her excitement was a physical presence in the room.

I said, "I wish you could hear yourself, the confidence and determination in your voice. Why don't you just forget the damn books? You already know how to rebuild. Make your lists, act on them, follow your instincts. You can do it, and we'll help, but I won't teach."

BJ's face glowed with pride. She was back on the right track, and all was well with whatever world we had. But I still had one question.

"What is this about body fat?"

"Oh, hell, I forgot to tell you. I figured out why women survived. Body fat. Women have a higher percentage of body fat."

"Nancy's not fat, and I'm just big-boned."

"Skinny women still have more body fat, percentage-wise, than even skinny men."

"Then why didn't *all* the women survive?"

"Some kind of resistance, immunity, or something."

Nancy joined in the game. "What about Rich? He survived. Where's his body fat?"

I knew.

"Between his ears."

We spent the following weeks making plans. BJ's enthusiasm was contagious. Finally, when she urged my partnership, I agreed. Traveling with her, rounding up strays, was infinitely more appealing than watching Nancy watch George. She'd started calling him Gig, with soft *g*'s, like Jij.

She and BJ debated the practicality of Rich's inevitable visit.

"One of them books said that lactation usually prevents conception."

"Usually isn't always, BJ. The same book said nursing should not be considered a reliable means of contraception. I might get pregnant again."

"Nan, are you sure that's what you want? Isn't it kinda soon? Georgie needs a lot of attention right now. Do you want to spread yourself that thin?" BJ reasoned.

"Look, if it doesn't work, it doesn't work. I'll just take that as a sign, but I think we ought to try. It's not like I can just give him a call, invite him over when the time is right. He comes when he comes." Nancy didn't see the humor in her last sentence, and looked questioningly at my snicker.

BJ was silent for a while, the first two fingers of her right hand working a parallel massage up and down her forehead, forcing thought. Finally she said, "OK, what if we get him to stay in town, we'll set him up in one of the houses. Then you can go to him, or we can send him out on assignment, something like that. What do you think?"

"That might work," Nancy said.

"I doubt it," I said. "In the first place, what makes you think he'll go for it?"

"First of all, he'll do it if I tell him to, and second of all, he's lazy. It'd appeal to his lazy egotism to have women coming to his door."

"I want to go back to the first-of-all. That's the second time you've suggested that you can make Rich do anything you want. What do you have on him, anyway?"

BJ smiled. "It isn't like that, Vic. It's not blackmail. It's just power. I've got it; he knows it."

"Aren't you concerned that once he's set up in town, he'll try to take over? He is a man, and a lot of the women would expect him to become the leader. They would accept his authority simply because he's male. How are you going to insure *your* power?" I looked at her.

"Power simply means the ability to achieve your goals, either by yourself, or by getting others to help. Rich doesn't even have any goals."

"How do you know that? How can you be so damned sure?"

"I've talked to him, plenty. He visited my house often. I picked his brain. He drank my beer."

There was something disturbing about the vision of Rich and BJ as drinking buddies. I could see them sitting at her formica and chrome kitchen table, the empties pyramided in the middle of the table, the open door from the kitchen into her bedroom. I shook off the thought. Impossible. BJ and

117

I were, well, a couple. We never promised each other fidelity. It seemed unnecessary in our decimated world. And she wouldn't sleep with a man, would she? Certainly not Rich. Although I knew I was being ridiculous, I could not shake the image of them, together, in her bed.

It was easy to forget that any of us had a life before we met. I'd forgotten that BJ'd been a married woman, that heterosexuality, the practice of it, had been the norm for most of her life. She loved me so well, so skillfully, and she loved Nancy, if only chastely, but she had been some man's wife. What was his name? Did she miss that kind of sex? Did she miss him?

I could not bear to think about it, and so of course I could think of nothing else. I struggled to superimpose a different mental image, to say something else.

"But what will you do if he tries to take over?"

BJ didn't hesitate. She looked me straight in the eye and said, "Get rid of him."

As BJ and I drove away, Nancy stood cradling her son. Her face wore an expression of guarded relief, as if this were the departure of loved but overstayed guests. One more glance over my shoulder showed her in a lazy barefooted waltz with the limbless George still swaddled in a hand-crocheted afghan.

It was spring with a vengeance. The grass was an unusual, defiant green, and there was so damned much of it. I don't know if there really was that much of a change in the foliage that spring or if it was just the first time I lifted my eyes from the narrowness of our three-cornered life, but either way the effect was awesome.

Our driveway was gone, the quackgrass and dandelions had reclaimed their birthright. There were only four patches where the tires had inhibited growth, and in the double path where we backed out, already the green was springing back. The dirt road was almost completely overgrown, with knee-high weeds stroking the truck as we drove past.

As we turned onto the paved road, BJ and I simultaneously swore.

Mine was a vulgarity. Hers, a blasphemy. Nancy would have scolded, but she was behind us. Ahead of us the road was marked, section by section, outlined in green. Every crack sprouted some vigorous growing thing. Potholes were dish gardens. Some joints were pushed up like miniature mountain ranges, sprouting vegetation. There was a tiny elm, maybe a foot high, directly in front of us. BJ swerved to miss it. I looked over at her and she grimaced.

"Seems like a shame to hurt anything that wants to live so bad it pokes itself through cement."

"Concrete. Cement is what they use ... *used* to make concrete."

"Whatever," she grumbled. Then she gestured wordlessly toward the passing landscape. Poison oak snaked up the purposeless utility poles, wild grapevines wound diagonally up guy wires. Fences were obscured by climbing, clinging, aggressive

119

greenery, where fences stood at all. Houses stared blankly, porches, steps, even occasional roofs coated in vines, grasses, moss.

Foot-high dandelions struggled to bloom above the surrounding grasses. Forsythia bushes, just past their prime, looked bruised, dejected. Clumps of lilacs were beginning to blossom in dark purples, lavenders, and, less frequently, white. Long arms of spirea stretched out. Once in a while we could see just a quick glimpse of color, tulips maybe or early roses, through militant weeds and tentative trees.

Patiently and persistently, nature it seemed had finally won its war against hedge-trimming, grass-clipping, rototilling, wood chip-mulching, and Weed-B-Gone.

The overgrowth was even more astonishing as we got closer to town. BJ or I would point out some new sight and the other would nod acknowledgment while we scanned the roadside. We barely spoke.

Town was more of the same, something green growing in every conceivable crevice, sidewalks almost completely obscured, privet hedges spread unchecked in all directions. Nobody's yard was better kept than any other. Branches blown down in winter or spring storms littered the street; twice we had to get out to move limbs too large to drive over. Three autumns' worth of unraked leaves decomposed quietly. One of the stained-glass windows in the Methodist church was shattered; an overachieving clump of dandelions grew on the sill.

As we turned onto Main Street, we were both startled to hear a bell clang several times, the last note hanging in the air like an unkept promise.

"What the hell?" was all that BJ said.

Two more blocks and I pointed out the answer. BJ's tiny front yard was neatly trimmed. Clustering around the step was a group of women, fifteen or twenty of them, smiling and waving wildly at us. One of them ran onto the porch, grabbed an iron wand, and struck a rusted iron triangle which hung from a porch rafter on a length of vinyl clothesline.

BJ beamed back a grin and jumped from the still-rolling truck. She was grabbed and hugged, everyone jabbering at once. I heard her deep voice through the din as I walked in the wake of her welcome. She named each woman, asking questions.

"Carol, did that finger heal good? Ruthann, got any rhubarb sauce made up? Maureen. You look great, winter okay?"

On and on.

I'd never thought of these people as friends of hers. She never mentioned them by name; she referred to then as "folks," the "town" or even "the zombs." But clearly she was someone special to them. I was ignored. She didn't even introduce me. A flash of jealousy, childish but real, stung my face like windburn.

BJ was moving through the crowd toward her front steps. When she reached them, the women became silent. I eased to BJ's side. There, sitting on the bottom step, one of the women, a young one, was holding a bundle. The pose was classic. It didn't take brilliance to figure out what was in her arms.

"Sandy," said BJ in a fond whisper. "Let me see."

She held her bundle up to BJ. "It's a girl, BJ. But ..."

"Hush," said my friend and lover as she unwrapped the child. There was a shifting movement as the group shot questioning glances at one another.

A corner of the blanket shadowed the child's face, and BJ moved it away last.

Unlike George, this child had all its body parts, all the required allotment of arms and legs, fingers and toes. But the little body hunched upward on its right side, its right hip and shoulder several inches higher than its left, eyes almost touching, mouth completely on the left half of its face, its right ear where the cheekbone should be. The almost-joined eyes twinkled, its left-sided mouth twitched up in an unmistakable smile, and its hand clutched BJ's finger.

Its mother spoke. "I named her Jane. Is that all right?"

BJ handed the child back and, looking deeply into Sandy's eyes, she traced her jawline with one finger, then caught her chin and tilted her face up. BJ whispered, "Sure," just before she kissed Sandy fully on the mouth.

CHAPTER 17

Until I was maybe fifteen, I read the word *pubic* as having an *l* in the middle, which was pretty confusing, that illogical name for something that was supposed to be private.

I was also the last of the cousins to believe in Santa Claus and the Easter Bunny, and as for elves, gnomes and leprechauns, well, I still harbor hope.

So it is possible that I read into BJ something that was never there, that I gave up my fantasy only when forced to.

As she worked that crowd, slick as a politician

up for reelection, I marveled at my naïveté, my love-blindness. I was angry and hurt and jealous, good emotions for clearing one's vision.

The way a kaleidoscope clicks as jagged bits of cheap glass are rearranged and reflected to appear as something wondrous, something special, reality clicked almost audibly in my reluctant ear.

I saw my BJ as a user and manipulator of people, ambitious for only God knows what kind of power in this condensed world. I saw myself as her dupe, her lackey, her yes ma'am. Just keep me coming and I keep going. Led by my libido as these others were led by — what? Loneliness? Insecurity? Desperation? And Nancy, I thought, dear Nancy, living as not much more than a brood sow, serviced by a less than ideal stud.

And our attempt to survive this enigmatic plague, maybe even to rise above the devastation of our comfortable lives, was something worse than sad. It was laughable. We weren't brave pioneers carving out a new world, and we weren't emigrants in a better place. We were just a handful of pathetic nomads whose demise was being delayed a bit longer than the others. We were flukes, denied by resistant genes the privilege of quick death.

The town was deteriorating, structures made by human hands taking themselves apart with a little help from gravity and wind and rain. Metal rusted, wood shed paint, leaves and broken-off limbs of trees lay where they fell or were blown. The neatly clipped grass in front of BJ's house, done as an honor, seemed ludicrous now, slightly obscene, a shaven pubic display.

And I felt a fool.

* * * * *

BJ kept talking to them. She sat on the porch
and used their names and touched them, hugged and
kissed them as I stood awkwardly nearby. She didn't
look at me, didn't introduce me, didn't wave me to
her side where I thought I belonged. It was rude
and it was cruel. How could I have become an
afterthought only two hours after I lay in her arms?
I listened to them, but there was nothing I wanted
to hear.

I turned away. I gave up needing or wanting
explanations or introductions. I rejected the comfort
knowledge can bring. Instead, I went exploring,
something I'd never done before, when I'd been as
busy with BJ as she was now with these women. I
walked up and over and down the streets, many
only a block long and none of them one-way, not
that that would have stopped me. Sometimes I would
step up onto a porch, sometimes into a house, but
there was a damp coldness I could feel in my bones
that repelled me. There was plenty of time for
rummaging through dead people's effects. I hurried
back into the sunlight.

Occasionally, I would find a house that one or
more of the women lived in. They looked like the
empty ones from the outside, but inside that
coldness was gone. They hadn't needed BJ to tell
them which houses to pick; the lived-in ones each
had a fireplace or a wood-burning stove. In one, a
stack of broken furniture was piled almost to the
ceiling by the fireplace. In another, blankets and
quilts were nailed to the walls. One house had

125

firewood chopped and stacked around the outside foundation. But the logs were not very thick. I was sure they wouldn't burn long, that more energy was expended in chopping and stacking those narrow loglets than they would ever return.

It was a quaint town, Main Street being the main street, three churches at the corner of Main and Church, School Street ending with the elementary and middle schools facing each other across a square. It would be another two years before I found the high school, built three miles from the town center.

Some of the roads were named for other towns' names, and I was pretty sure that they would eventually lead to their namesakes.

Finally on the north side of town, two blocks from Main Street, were the village's northern boundaries. I realized there was a sound, a noise, that I'd been unconsciously drawn to.

There was water, not like a river, really, but more than a trickle coming from the east and collecting in a pond behind a small factory that, judging from the For Sale signs, had been empty long before the town was. A concrete dam created the pond, the overflow washing over the top. I followed the stream and in less than a block came to what had been a park. It still was, sort of.

The water pump that BJ had told me about was in the center, and the beaten grass and muddy earth showed where the women came for their water. But the swings and slide were rusty and rickety, self-demolishing from disuse.

One of the swings was moving in a breeze I

could not feel. I retraced my steps to where the stream trickled under School Street.

And then I noticed what I hadn't before. Solidly standing at the corner of School and (what else?) Water streets was a rectangular brick building. An apartment building, one story up and one down, half in the ground. Patio doors opened from the back of the building into the yard which ended shortly in the stream, just before it emptied into the pond.

The door slid open without too much effort and I entered the first downstairs apartment. In the corner, left of the door, was a shiny black inverted funnel that I recognized. It was a wood burner, purely decorative, I judged by the lack of a stove pipe, but capable of functioning. I stepped back outside to examine the exterior wall. It was brick, but brick can be broken. I could break through and run a pipe up ... I was planning the how of it when it dawned on me what I was doing. It was a surprise. I was planning to make this my home. Mine and no one else's. I wandered through the rooms, two bedrooms, one tiny bathroom, the room I'd entered into from outside tripling as kitchen and dining and living rooms. I tried to figure out why I'd felt so instantly at home here. The furniture was nice, the solid wood tables finished in natural tones, the sofa upholstered in beige leather, real leather. There were two chrome-and-leather chairs, the sort I never would have chosen but which were, when I sat in one, surprisingly comfortable. The framed pictures, askew and needing cleaning, as did everything in there, were original works, not famous or anything, but real watercolors and acrylics and oils.

Later I would learn they were painted by friends and family of their former owner and acquired with no more money than it cost for mass-produced reprints, once available at any discount department store. There were books in bookcases designed by the owner and made by a friend in exchange for restoring an antique quilt. There were lots of books, on many subjects, one shelf of which were all autographed by their authors, friends of my predecessor. But I wouldn't find out those details until later, when I found her journals.

I walked through the rooms again, trying to pinpoint my attraction to the place, thinking of the cleaning I would have to do to make it habitable, thinking how to clean the carpet, when realization dawned. It was the carpet. In all the rooms it was the same. The carpet was a lovely pale sea-green I knew so well. Celadon. Celadon, the color I'd always believed, of my soul. I took off my shoes and walked on it barefoot, then I lay on it, stretching like a cat. A cat. All I needed was a cat to stretch out with on celadon.

CHAPTER 18

I fell asleep on that carpet with my head pillowed on my arms, and woke so rested that I knew I really had come home.

Searching the closets and under the sinks, I found a broom, a pail, some household cleaner. I swept the carpet with the broom, an exhausting but effective exercise. Then out the open patio door went the dirt.

How does an empty house get dirty? The question of the ages.

Half-filling the bucket at the stream, I poured in

cleaner and attacked the surfaces. Cleaning BJ's house had been like sifting through the rubble of destruction. And Nancy did most of the cleaning at the farm. This apartment was mine. I cleaned with care, freshening the water several times. I was almost finished, not only because the apartment was clean but because nightfall was coming fast, when I heard a deep-throated chuckle at the door.

BJ said, "So here you are, sweetie. I was getting worried. Why'd you take off like that?"

My anger and disillusion had cooled with my working and my joy at finding a home. I actually smiled.

"Beej, look, look what I found. A place of my own," I blurted, not thinking how it sounded.

For a whole beat longer than was comfortable, she stood there with her eyes narrowed. I realized I'd excluded her without even thinking. Excuses flooded my mind, but all I really could think was that this apartment was mine. I didn't want anyone else living there, no matter who. An image of her messes strewn across my carpet, my furniture, horrified me. As I groped for something diplomatic to say, she finally spoke.

"Well, I guess that's your decision. I kinda understand. And besides . . ." She stopped and narrowed her eyes again. "I guess there's nothing harder to move than a woman who's found where she wants to be. C'mon. Ain't you hungry? We're having a party. You've already contributed. I passed around the eggs Nancy sent in with you. You shoulda seen how excited they were to see eggs! I'm going out to the farm and get Nance to donate some chickens to these townies. I shoulda thought of that before."

She rambled on as I reluctantly closed the door behind us and started walking with her toward her house.

Suddenly I remembered this had been her hometown. She'd lived there all her life. She must have known the woman who lived in my apartment before me.

"Wait a minute, Beej, you . . . did you know her?" I pulled her arm to stop her feet.

"Know who?"

"Her. The one who used to live in my house."

She looked down at me. There was still enough light left to see a twinkle in her eyes.

"You too, huh?"

"Me too what?"

"You fell in love with her too, and you never even met her. That figures." She turned and started walking away, knowing for sure I'd follow.

"Her name was Anne and no one called her Annie," said BJ.

"She moved here after a divorce, four, maybe five years before, well, you know. Before. Nobody knew much about her, so of course everyone pretended to. The stories grew wilder and wilder. She'd been married seven times, she'd made movies, she'd been around the world, she spoke six languages — actually, that last one was true. Some said she was a reformed prostitute, some said she wasn't reformed. Some said she was rich, or her daddy was and that was how she could live like she did. Some said she was gay — that one was half right. Few know the truth about Anne. But I did."

I was silent, listening.

"She took a job at the movie rental place, but it seemed odd. She was smarter and classier than that job. It didn't pay much and she always looked so, well . . . above that. Not that she acted like she was. It was just something about the way she carried herself, about the way she talked and moved. The way she gave her attention to you when you talked to her. That's where I met her and how I got to know her, but I'll tell you more another time, because here we are and there are some alive people you need to know."

But I couldn't let it go at that. I just had to know. "You mean she isn't? Alive, I mean. Did you, did you bury her too?"

"Nope. I did not. She was out of town when it happened. Chicago or someplace. Not that I believe she's still alive. I think I'd know it, feel it somehow, if she was." BJ turned and looked at me. "See, I kinda loved her too. Everybody did in one way or another. Even the ones that hated her loved her. They hated her because she didn't want their love, anyone's love. Didn't allow people to get as close to her as she got to them. She never asked any questions, but people just always talked to her. Told her stuff they didn't tell anyone else. That scared some people, especially since she never opened up to them. But when she'd smile, you'd forget that you had no idea who she was or what she wanted. You'd just pour out your guts some more. And then, too, she never fucked anybody. People didn't understand that. If she'd screwed around they would have pretended to be shocked, but they would have understood her as being human. They would have accepted her better. You know how people are. They sort of like feeling better than someone else. They like them better if they feel that that liking is some kind of gift they can give to someone less deserving." Her voice had picked up a bitter edge to it. I wasn't sure she was still talking about Anne.

I asked, "So you're saying you never slept with her?"

"Goddammit, Vic, you are the most jealous person I ever met. I just told you she never slept with nobody, at least not in this town. Every once in a while she'd go off to Chicago. Maybe she had someone out there. I don't know! Hell's bells, woman. Even I don't fuck everyone I'd like to! Besides, that was Before. What do you care who I screwed before I even knew you? Get off my tit!" BJ strode toward the group of women now in sight. As I followed, suspecting she was less angry than she made out, I thought about how she was right about my being jealous, but wrong about who I was jealous of. I was so relieved that my Anne had never slept with BJ.

As we'd walked toward her house, I'd seen a light growing brighter and brighter. In the middle of the road in front of her house stood, incredibly, a barbecue grill. One of the women — I later found out her name was Carol — was poking at something with a long-handled fork. In addition, there were two other grills, also tended. One had a large pot on it and the other had a smaller one. Something smelled unbelievably delicious. I peeked into the smaller pot after shooting a quick smile at the woman standing nearby.

Inside the pot were, I guessed, all three dozen of the eggs Nancy had sent.

The woman, whose name I would soon learn was Maureen, shot a delighted grin at me.

"BJ says your friend Nancy sent these. Thank you. Thank her. Thank God. Fresh eggs! My God, fresh eggs!" She wiped her eyes.

Eggs were no treat to me, I'd lived on them for three years. But I just smiled at her and moved to peer into the next pot.

It was soup, with a few bits of vegetables and a lot of broth, but it smelled good. The woman stirring it lifted a spoon for me to taste it, but all I could identify was an overdose of pepper.

She laughed when I sputtered, then said, "I tried growing vegetables last summer. This is all that's left. This year I'm trying potatoes and carrots and onions only. Now that will be a soup."

BJ sidled up to me then and gave my waist a quick squeeze. "I see you've met Bernice."

Still unable to catch my breath after that taste of soup, I nodded at the woman, meaning hello, but BJ took it as assent and pulled me toward the third grill.

"This here's Carol. Carol, this is Vic. Vic, this is rabbit," said BJ.

"Pleased to meet you," I said, addressing the

grilling meat. Carol laughed and stuck out her hand for me to shake.

"Welcome, and stand back, this stuff spatters."

"These are Carol's rabbits," said BJ. "She raises them."

"And kills and cleans them?"

"And eats 'em," said Carol.

"Where'd you learn a skill like that?" I asked.

"Taught myself, two summers ago. The first few were a mess, but I got the hang of it."

"You should see how she raises them," said BJ with pride. "She keeps them in a box with a chicken wire top and bottom and moves them around every day. They eat the grass."

"I have to move them every day or they'd dig out. I learned that the hard way, too. All I have to do is give them water. I'm trying to learn to tan their skins, too, but haven't got it just right yet." Carol wrinkled her nose. "I'm still working on it."

"Here comes the wine!" BJ pointed to a woman headed our way with a wheelbarrow.

"And the greens!" called another woman walking beside her carrying a plastic bag.

BJ performed the introductions to Joan, the wine-bearer, and Betty. "This is Vic, my ... friend. My pal."

Betty thrust her bag at me and I peered inside. It was full of young, tender dandelion greens. Joan pulled a jar from her wheelbarrow and handed it to Betty who held it up for me to see.

"White vinegar and chive flowers," Betty said, "the best salad dressing ever known to man."

Joan looked quickly from side to side and crowed, "Man? What man?" They both laughed and walked toward BJ's porch, where more women waited with glasses and plates.

Picnic tables — from where? — had been dragged onto the lawn and another fire, presumably for illumination only, burned in a steel drum in the driveway.

There were more names and more varieties of food. Tough biscuits and canning jars of applesauce.

I wished for just a minute that Nancy'd been there, until I remembered my little apartment waiting for me. I didn't think Nancy would have accepted my newfound independence as quickly as BJ had. Someone with a guitar sat on the porch steps picking out half-songs and phrases, never finishing any of them.

The girl named Sandy danced with her infant, a dance with no pattern, just slipping and slipping.

BJ joined them, putting her arms around both and resting her cheek in Sandy's curls.

I poured another glass of wine from the jug and listened to Joan tell how she gathered up all the alcohol in town, door to door, store to store, and kept it all at her house.

I listened to all the voices and tried to make sense of the conversation.

Without any emotion, I watched BJ cuddle Sandy. Then someone shouted, "Look, oh my God, look!" and we all looked. There were tiny sparks of light darting here and there and blinking on and off.

"Lightning bugs!" someone else shouted, then everyone laughed and started trying to catch them and put them in their glasses.

Everyone except BJ and Sandy and me, that is. I remembered what BJ had said about a woman finding a home and I realized she wasn't just talking about me in Anne's apartment.

Sandy looked up at BJ with such devotion that all I wanted to do was to stumble home. My home. Alone.

CHAPTER 19

The dandelion salad gave me diarrhea.

I fertilized the hell out of the line of forsythia at the other end of my building. It was hard to believe there was that much in me to shit out. I wondered if I was shitting body parts, and I had dry cramps long after there was nothing left in me.

Between that and the wine hangover — I hadn't drunk that much, but it had been a long time — I didn't really sleep until dawn and slept very late. I drank only water for the rest of the day, and lay on the sofa, cocooned in Anne's afghan, feeling sorry for myself but safe.

Maureen and Betty stopped by with leftover salad, wilted now. I was polite but I didn't encourage future visits and after they left I dumped the greens with their hurriedly digested predecessors.

BJ never showed up, and I tried not to feel miffed. No doubt she had her hands full — her mouth too, I suspected.

It didn't take long for a pattern to emerge in our village life — actually, I just kept to myself. At one time or another all the women came over, and I tolerated rather than welcomed their neighborliness.

Except for Maureen, that is. Maureen I welcomed. Always.

It was, still is, impossible to pinpoint her age, and I never asked. Maybe she was twenty years older than I was. She had pure white hair that grew in gentle waves. Short, maybe not even five feet tall, she had pink, firm skin and blue eyes that could twinkle benevolently or flare with outrage.

We trusted each other instinctively, but still took our time building a friendship. We were like-minded in many ways, and in the ways we weren't, we companionably agreed to disagree.

She knew me for what I was, my relationship with BJ no surprise. She said the word straight out.

"You're a lesbian, aren't you?"

"Uh huh. Does that bother you?"

"Not in the least. BJ is too, I assume. Are you and she lovers?"

"Have been. Past tense, apparently."

"Why do you say that?"

"Well, there's Sandy, for one. Her attitude since we got to town for another. Just a feeling I have, I guess."

"What does Sandy have to do with it?"

"Didn't you see them together our first night here? That seemed pretty clear to me. Plus, she never comes around."

"Have you been to see her?"

"No. I just figured I'd have to see her and Sandy together some more, so . . ." I shrugged.

"Sandy doesn't live with her. She shares a house with Carol. Sandy isn't a lesbian. I don't think she and BJ — well, I think you may be wrong. Why don't you talk to her? Discuss this."

"She knows where I live, how to find me."

"Vic, I know I haven't known you very long, and maybe I should keep my opinions to myself, but that's something I've never been able to do, so I guess it's too late to start now. This is no time to stop communicating. Now seems to be the perfect time to learn to talk openly and honestly with each other. Talk to your BJ. Then listen when she talks. We all have to do this. We have to! We're all we've got left."

Maureen's blue eyes paled as tears filled her eyes. She had a story, too, a life. She'd lost her family and friends, I was sure, but all I'd done on our visits was talk about me.

She shamed me with her graciousness. I tried to comfort her. She let me awkwardly hold her. Then she pulled away and wiped her face with a no-nonsense gesture I would come to know very well.

Stopping on her way out the door, she turned and shook her finger at the naughty child, me.

"You talk to your friend. I mean it," she said.

But of course I didn't, not for a while at least. Not until BJ came to me.

It seems so childish now, looking back on it, but I was younger then, and so sure I was right, so sure that since I was right, BJ must be wrong.

So she stood at my door and knocked, actually knocked like a stranger on the glass of the patio door which I used as my front entrance. Even now I've never used the real front door with its fisheye peephole.

She was uneasy, uncomfortable with me. I grabbed a cloth and started dusting an undusty table to avoid looking at her. She looked miserable. Her misery showed me my own.

I stopped dusting and small-talking.

"I've missed you, BJ," I said, but I didn't move toward her.

"Oh God, Vic, I've missed you too. What's wrong? Why don't you want me anymore?"

She sank to the sofa, with her head between her hands, her shoulders shaking. Was my strong, capable BJ crying? I went to her, knelt on the floor at her feet and lifted her head.

Tears streamed down her blotchy face, her eyes were swollen and red-rimmed, her nose was runny, and she sniffled between words.

"How can you be done with me just like that? Dammit, Vic, I thought we had something."

"Beej," I said wiping her face with the hem of my T-shirt, raising it above my midriff to reach her. "Beej, don't. Don't do this. God. I can't bear this. To see you like this. Don't, please don't."

She touched my bare skin with the back of her

hand as she grabbed the waist of my jeans and pulled me closer. "Vic, I need you. I need *us*."

It was such a simple gesture but so powerful, so arousing, I forgot all about the silent weeks behind us, about Sandy, and about Maureen's admonitions. I forgot everything except how good making love with BJ was. We cleared the air with action and reaction.

She spent the night, and in the morning, over a breakfast of ancient raisins, I decided to take the plunge.

"What about Sandy?"

"Sandy can get her own breakfast," smart-assed BJ.

I punched her semi-playfully on the arm. "I'm serious. You made me jealous as hell with all that snuggling."

"Good. I meant to. It's good to feel jealous every once in a while. Reminds you who you care about."

"What!" I choked on a raisin. "You deliberately made me jealous? You bitch!"

"Me? I'm a bitch? What about you, Little Miss Who's-a-Dyke?"

"What about *you*? We cross the village limits and you forget my name?"

"I can understand someone wanting to keep her private life private, but dammit anyway, Vic. You. Can. Be. Cold. Why'd you just sit in the truck like that when we got here? Why didn't you join us? I wanted to introduce you around. I wanted everyone to know that we're a couple. That you're mine. That, that ... well, that I'm not just a ... a ... pal. That someone wants me in a sex way. I want them to know that someone special — and that *is* you — thinks I am someone special and not just a big old ... pal. And there you sit, ignoring me. Shit! How do you think I felt?"

She didn't even know I hadn't waited in the truck. That made me madder than anything, but typically, I threw back at her everything but that.

"What the fuck are you talking about? Me? *Me* ignore *you?* Excuse me, Madam Mayor, I'm the ignored one here. I was good enough for you when there wasn't anyone else, but here in Metropolis where your word is law and you can pick and choose, suddenly I'm invisible? Or don't they know what you are? Don't you want them to know how you get yours? Are you afraid they won't worship you if they know you fuck women?"

Looking thoughtful, not angry anymore, she asked, "What did you call me?"

She lost me. My turn to be confused. I thought we were getting somewhere. I hadn't even gotten to the manipulator part, and she was off on some tangent.

"BJ, we need to finish this, don't get sidetracked. Let's fight."

She smiled crookedly and waved away my words. "Nah, we can finish this some other time. Besides, we made up already. What did you call me?"

"Bitch, for one. Dyke. User. Phony. I hadn't gotten around to cunt-lapper, but ..."

"No. Not those. Madam Mayor. That's why I came here last night. That was my excuse if you weren't glad to see me. We're going to have a meeting. We have a lot to discuss. I've been taking notes. I want you to be there. Tonight, at sundown. First we're going to have another group meal. Bring anything you can find, or nothing, just none of these raisins. Come, okay?"

"See? You only need me to come for you." I leered.

"Or when I need to." She stood and held her hand out to me in cavalier fashion.

I rose and curtsied, putting my hand in hers and letting her lead me back to bed.

Abrupt mood swings are hell on my libido.

CHAPTER 20

We did agree not to live together. It wasn't a separation, at least we didn't think so at the time. And we didn't care if the others knew about us. We preferred it, we agreed, but I wanted to stay in Anne's apartment and BJ wanted to stay in her house.

We decided to visit freely and sleep over whenever we felt like it. We discussed altering our living arrangements for winter, so only one place would have to be heated. But winter seemed far away and neither of us dreamed how far apart we would be by then.

After BJ left, I took the shovel I found in the prefab tool shed and went to the far end of the building to dig a latrine for myself. Then I went around back, which was really the front of the building, and started turning over the earth for my own vegetable garden; Betty had also brought me some seeds.

It was slow, hard work, but those rectangles between the sidewalks and the parking lot got full sun and seemed ideal for a garden.

I was only half finished when I noticed the sun lowering. Stripping, I washed in the icy cold stream, then ran naked inside to find something appropriate to wear to a dinner party/political rally.

Anne's taste in clothes was offbeat, and she must have been pretty tiny — must be, I mean — but I found a purple caftan that I felt spiffy in. After all, I thought, it's not as if there are any current fashions to flout.

My shoes looked silly with the caftan and Anne's were all too small, so I went barefoot up to the neighbor's and borrowed a pair of pink rubber thongs we used to call flip-flops. Scoping out the upstairs apartment was one of the ways I'd spent the last couple of weeks, and I'd remembered seeing shoes that looked my size. On my way out, the setting sun's rays reflected off something in a half-open utility closet.

Folding open the doors, I found three eight-packs of brown gold. Three years old, at least, and warm and dusty and beautiful. Pepsi. It felt like falling in love.

I grabbed one eight-pack and took it to the stream, plunging the cans to the bottom.

Then I walked empty-handed to dinner, but I'd be back to fetch dessert. Cold and clear and biting, and just before the meeting. I figured I was a shoo-in for vice mayor.

This time, Carol and Betty had worked together and made rabbit stew, with dumplings, yet.

Sandy was there with her baby, which she nursed openly with her shapeless breasts. Once I believed there was nothing between her and BJ, I could pretend to admire her godawful-looking child. Sandy was a dull, uninteresting woman with whom it was impossible to converse. She answered questions with monosyllabic grunts and never looked me in the eye. Not once. At least not that night. It was disconcerting, until I noticed that she behaved like this toward everyone. It wasn't just me.

The others basically treated her like a pet, a cocker spaniel maybe. They'd pat her on the head and murmur little phrases that really did sound like "good girl" and "atta girl."

Maureen was there. I was glad to see her. She hugged me quickly and brought me a cup of the herb tea she'd brewed in a glass jug in the sun.

"Maureen," I said, "what's your last name?"

I should have known better. There is no such thing as small talk with Maureen. "Good morning" is an invitation to philosophy.

"I could tell you that," she answered after a

pause, "but what would it mean to you? Is there more than one Maureen here? For all we know, I'm the last Maureen in the world, the only one. Last names were invented when there got to be too many people with the same first name. Did you ever hear of Adam or Eve having last names? Last names identified people by what they did for a living or where they came from or who their parents were. And for women they meant which man they belonged to, father then husband. It was always an unfair system. My last name belonged to my husband, who got it from his father, who got it from his father. I never had the chance to pick any of my names. Shouldn't I get that chance? I like my name, Maureen, but what if I didn't? Tough luck. That's all. So now I'm just Maureen. Thank you very much. I'm Maureen the first! or Maureen the last . . ."

"Or Maureen the feisty," I finished for her.

She laughed, ire turned to embarrassment.

"I guess I got carried away. I'm sorry," she said.

"Don't ever apologize for being what you are. You're beautiful when you're indignant."

"Are you flirting with me?"

"No ma'am. I have given up flirting with you heteros. It is just a waste of time."

"You've guessed my little secret, have you?"

"From the start. I'm not always sure when someone is gay, but I'm always sure when they're not."

"I wondered about that," she said, no longer teasing. "It must be difficult. Have you ever been wrong? I mean, have you ever . . ."

"Come on to a straight person? Sure, I've even been in love with one or two. But really, is it that different for straights? Haven't you ever wanted someone who didn't want you? Haven't you ever thought someone was interested when they weren't, or at least not in the same way you were?"

"Sure," Maureen said. "It was embarrassing, and painful."

"Well, there you go. Me too." I thought of Nancy. Martha — only, with her, maybe if there'd been time . . .

Maureen was talking again. "So, at what point do you know for sure that the person, the woman, you want is really gay too?"

"When we're in bed together. After."

BJ came up behind me, and kissed me on the shoulder.

"I see you two have met. You look as thick as thieves. Do I have any reason to worry here?"

Her public kiss threw me and her banter sounded like there was a sharp edge buried just beneath the surface.

Maureen saved the moment by saying, "You probably saved my life by bringing Vic to us. I didn't think I'd ever again meet anyone I could really talk to. The trouble is, once I start I can't seem to stop. You'd better feed your woman before she drowns in my chatter, or starves to death."

I blew her a kiss as BJ led me away.

Maureen was the first straight person I'd ever met who didn't condemn, judge, avoid, confront or try to reform me.

She was also the first woman besides my mother whom I loved totally but not erotically. It was confusing and — what? Enlightening. An emancipation of some sort.

Until that year, until Maureen, love had always had romantic and/or erotic implications. Love meant being in love.

But trying to imagine making love to her seemed obscene. Something as repulsive as incest. But *love* was the only word for my feelings for her, right from the start. So love needed wider definition.

And Maureen was just the beginning. The end of summer would bring even more amazements.

But that night, there was rabbit stew, Pepsi surprise, and BJ's first step toward becoming queen of our world.

It was informal, to say the least. We stayed around the steel drum, for light and camaraderie.

Appropriately, BJ spoke first.

"We are here, all of us, because somehow we survived what many others didn't. We may never know what happened. Maybe it's better that way. Maybe not having anyone to blame will save us the energy and time we will need to continue surviving. There's still a lot of canned goods at the store — although, as we've seen tonight — we've already begun to find ways to provide for some of our own needs. This is good. I'm proud of all of you. I'm proud of us." She paused. "We've survived three winters which means we can probably survive more. We've kept from any serious arguments. That's impressive in a village full of women."

Several chuckles punctuated her talk.

"We've even proved there will be a next generation, a future."

Sandy smiled at this singling out of her maternity.

"We've formed some impressive friendships; we've helped each other through some bad times. And all of that is good. But the time has come for us to progress beyond survival. It is time for us to decide the shape of our future. We do not have to accept anything that has gone before. We can and must define our world. There are changes, small adjustments, that will be easy to make now, in this beginning, which will mean more than survival for all of us and for any who join us. We are the beginning, my friends, so let us begin."

"Hear, hear," several women intoned.

"Let's meet weekly to make mutual decisions about our own welfare. I would like to take this first week to make sure we have a list of resources, a kind of census of who's here and what talents and abilities we each have to contribute. I would like Vic to document these resources, if she would . . ."

She hadn't warned me, hadn't asked or even hinted about this angle. The women all stared at me — intelligent-looking, no doubt, with my mouth hanging open — then they literally applauded BJ's suggestion.

I had no objections to what she proposed, but I was pissed that she hadn't discussed it with me first.

"Of course, BJ, whatever I can do to help," I said.

Then she dropped the other bomb-shaped shoe. "For those of you who don't know — and I'm pretty sure you all know — Vic and I are lesbians. We are also a couple. Vic was a schoolteacher and may be

151

again some day" — this with a smile at Sandy and a pointed avoidance of my glare. "The most important thing I can say about starting fresh is that we have the opportunity to be totally honest with ourselves and with one another. It will save a lot of time and energy in the long run if we all know and accept where we all stand. I hate lies and I hate secrets. I'm not going to lie to you and I won't keep any secrets from you." Some of the women nodded their approvals. "Good night and don't forget to stop by Vic's and get this all started."

Another round of applause and BJ was shepherding me into her house.

"Well, what did you think?" she had the audacity to ask.

I could only stare at her for a minute, then said, "Spoken like a true politician, Beej. And to think you said all that without a single obscenity."

She missed my sarcasm completely.

"Yeah, I tried real hard. Jeez damn, I'm good! Take off that robe thing and let me show you how good I can be."

"Just wait one minute, okay? Why did you do that? Why didn't you tell me what you were planning to say? Why didn't you ask me how I felt about any of that?"

She waved away my questions as if they were a cloud of pesky fruit flies.

"What's wrong with what I said? You didn't have to agree to help."

"I wanted to agree to help before you tell the world I'm going to. And I think you could have left out the part about our personal lives. What was that about?"

"Well, actually, I hadn't planned to say that. It just seemed like a good idea at the time. Like an inspiration. You know, to show how up-front I'm willing to be with them."

"So you're saying it seemed like a good idea to humiliate me by exposing our relationship publicly so they would be impressed with your integrity?"

"Yeah, I guess, sort of. What's wrong with that?"

"You really can't see it? You really think what you did was okay?"

"Sure. You don't?"

Calm down. I became so calm. "No, BJ. No, ma'am, I do not."

And again I went home and slept alone.

CHAPTER 21

Maureen the Feisty was at my door early the next morning. Her look of concern touched me.

"Are you all right?" she asked.

"I guess so. Hurt again, surprised again, alone again. But okay."

"I've been worried about you all night. I saw your face. I felt bad for you."

"Thanks," I said. "I appreciate that. You're a good friend."

"Well, you might not think so when I tell you

that, up until the end, I was actually impressed with what she had to say, with how she handled herself. It may not sound very nice, but I really didn't know she had it in her to be so, well, so polished. The others were impressed too. And I was the only one who thought her ending was uncalled for."

So BJ had been right. Of course she had. How could I doubt it? I just sighed, and Maureen patted my hand.

After a while, she asked, "Vic, what does she want? Where is she going with all this? I don't mean to ask you to be disloyal to your friend, but it occurred to me that last night was not exactly a spur-of-the-moment occurrence. Can you talk about this, or would you rather not?"

I thought carefully before I answered.

"You know, she makes me crazy. Sometimes I feel so close to her and sometimes she seems like a total stranger."

"My husband was like that. We were married thirty-five years, and I was never sure what we were doing together. I guess that's one of the facets of love. Insecurity."

"What was his name?"

"No, no more past. We're talking about now and tomorrow. BJ. What does she want?"

"Power, I suppose, what all politicians want. She really does want to be able to bring about beneficial changes. I think she thinks almost constantly about how to improve whatever situation she's in. She cares about her people. You should see her with Nancy — Nancy is the girl, woman really, I live with, lived with. I'll tell you about her sometime.

But anyway, she found a way to give Nancy the only thing she wanted, a baby. She brought her a guy, this jerk named —"

"Not Rich?"

"Yeah, that's his name."

"Ugh, I've met him."

"So you know. But, he did the job."

"Where's Nancy now?"

"At the farm, just a few miles out of town, with her baby. Waiting for El Yucko's return."

"Does she care for him?"

"I don't think so, not really, but she's no fool. You know, never look a gift asshole in the mouth."

Maureen stifled a snicker. "Back to BJ. Do you trust her?"

"In our personal relationship, after last night, that's not a good question to ask. But as far as her views on what's best for the village — absolutely. You need to know I am personally opposed to the concept of organizing anything, and I've told her this over and over, that just letting things evolve naturally would be best and more interesting, too. On this we will never agree. But she's more determined to shape events than I am to resist her. And besides, as you have probably guessed, I love her. Even now. She's exciting and dependable and committed. She has so much energy, so much vision. I storm out her door, I shout and pout, I call her names and turn my back. And then I realize I've been wearing her socks, just to be near her, even though I'm angry. And she'll curl her finger, or smile, and I'm done for. I almost hate her for making me love her so much, especially when I don't always like her. And the worst part is that I don't know if she feels the same."

Maureen hugged me then, patting my head. "Yes, yes," she said. "Just like my husband." And as she left, she told me, "Just for your records, I was, am, a nurse. I taught nursing. I'll help out any way I can."

The women came to me in ones and twos, bringing their names and lists of talents. Some brought more: a jar of applesauce, tomato seeds, curiosity or trouble.

Sandy, who I'd decided to despise, left her childling with someone else and came to me that evening. She didn't seem to notice my distaste for her. She had the audacity to flirt with me.

"You're BJ's wife, aren't you?" she said. "Well, at least you're attractive. I can see why she wants you. You have great eyes."

"Wife?" I said, "I don't think of myself as her wife. Wife is like possession. I don't belong to her or vice versa."

"I didn't mean it as an insult, I mean, you're a couple, aren't you? Or do you date, or whatever, other people?"

An image of strangling the bitch formed in my mind with enyclopedic detail. I pondered the most effective position of the thumbs to perform the act.

She just rambled on. "I mean, do you, or would you, ever, or have you or could you, I mean, with say, someone like me? With me?"

I was so busy trying to control my homicidal urges, I didn't quite get what she was saying.

"I mean, I've been attracted to women sometimes, but you know I just never really, well, did anything much. Well, my cousin one summer when we were only ten. I mean, she was. I was eleven, but it was her idea and really we were just kind of, you know, touching and looking, but, don't you really think every girl's first experiment is with another girl? But I wouldn't mind. I mean, here we are, and I'm curious and I really like BJ and I know you're lovers or whatever but you don't live together so I thought maybe but, I mean, I don't know anything, you know, how to or anything, but I think I could learn."

There was no answer for her.

"Do you know what I mean?" she asked.

"I think so. You want to fuck BJ."

"Well, if that's the right word."

"It'll do. You want to fuck my woman and you want me to show you how?"

"Well, yeah, because you are one already."

"I are one what?" I wanted to hear her say the word, any of the words, the L word or the D word or the G word or the H word. I wondered what any of them would sound like coming out of her stupid mouth.

She just smiled. "Well, you know ..."

I rose slowly from my seat and walked to her until her face was inches from my navel. She didn't flinch as I reached behind her and grabbed a handful of her stringy hair into a rough ponytail, pulling her head back to look up at me. A shadow passed over her eyes, revealing some deep emotion that made my skin crawl.

"Let me give you some advice," I whispered, bending toward her. "Get the hell away from me and *stay* the hell away from me. If you ever lay even one finger on BJ, you little shit, I'm going to kill you. Do you understand me?"

I twisted the handful of hair until tears came to her eyes, but she never pulled away from me, never cried out.

"Do you understand me?" I asked again.

"Yes," she whispered. "Yes."

"Get out," I said as I released her.

She left without another word, without looking back. She shut the door behind her.

I wiped my hand on my pant leg as if some residue of our meeting was sticky on my fingers.

I knew even then that what I'd done was a mistake. That expression on her face when I'd hurt her told me how it was with her. I knew I'd done the one thing she'd come there for. She'd tricked me into it and I knew she'd be back and I knew BJ'd be with her. Damn.

She was going to succeed by being weak. That fucking ancient game.

Damn her and damn BJ and damn me too!

Well, I thought, at least I'm attractive! At least! ... I mean.

It didn't take long. The next morning they were

there, waiting for me when I got back from peeing in the forsythias.

BJ looked stern, controlled. Sandy half hid behind BJ's right shoulder with her eyes brimming with the tears she hadn't bothered to waste last night.

"I think we need to talk, Vic," said BJ. I didn't answer, so she continued, "Sandy says you tried to rape her last night."

"Rape her? Good God, Beej, you don't believe that, do you?" This was not the accusation I expected. Attempted murder, maybe. But murder can be justified. She was smarter, and more evil, than I'd thought.

BJ said, "Well, that's why I'm here. I want to hear your side of the story."

"There is no story, except for what this slug-shit made up. Goddamnit, BJ, you know me better than this. How could you believe her for even a second?"

"Just tell me what happened," she said.

"This slut came here last night asking me how to get into your bed. I threw her out. Period." BJ looked at Sandy and Sandy looked at BJ and then BJ looked at me. But Sandy never stopped looking at BJ, and with all that looking and not looking, I knew I'd lost. BJ knew I was telling the truth but it didn't matter, because I'd fallen in a trap I couldn't have avoided. Sandy'd gotten me to tell BJ what she couldn't: that she was willing. And even a liar can get laid.

BJ left with Sandy and I decided I would never let myself fall in love again. Never.

160

CHAPTER 22

For a long time I kept to myself, allowing only Maureen to visit me. She brought me news and vegetable seeds. There were more seeds than news.

She said I was depressed. I slept away God only knew how much time. Some days I would go out, intending to weed my scrawny garden, and just give up after a few handfuls.

Maureen fed me last fall's hickory nuts and fresh dandelion greens. My stomach had gotten used to them since that first barbecue. She brewed herb teas in the sun and generally kept me alive. She never said, "Snap out of it," or, for that matter, "There, there." She did, however say words sweet to my ear: "Everything will be all right," and "Just give it time."

Of course she was right. She was always right, damn-bless her.

One morning the sky seemed higher, and colors returned to my halftone world.

The sun felt warm again, though the summer'd been hot so far. I hadn't seen BJ in several weeks.

Maureen was experimenting with drying fruits and vegetables layered between window screens in the sun. She read books on edible wild greens and medicinal uses for plants.

Late one evening, as we stood lounging at the door, saying goodbyes and then thinking of just one more thing to say, and then just one more, a crackling in the brush across the brook caught our attention. A deer was drinking there. It seemed oblivious to us, and we just watched in awe as it drank. Half-turned away from us, it seemed so beautiful, so perfect.

Maureen reached out and held my hand. That slight motion caused the deer to look up at us. It stared for a few seconds, then turned and, instead of bolting, just sauntered away.

As it turned to leave, the side we couldn't see before was exposed and there, jutting out of the side of this lovely, tawny creature was the twisted fore and hind legs of what would, probably, have been its twin. Would have been if something hadn't gone horribly wrong.

Maureen choked back a sob and I reached for her. So strong and wise, she uttered three gasps, then pushed away from me and impatiently wiped her pale cheeks.

She turned to look at me and said, "That reminds me, I meant to ask you if you've ever done any hunting."

I hadn't, but figured I could learn. There was a sporting goods store two side streets over, still locked from closing time years before.

Breaking a window with a concrete block, I entered and browsed a while before finding the display of bows and arrows. Archery had always intrigued me, but I'd never had time before to pursue it.

There were guns in cases and plenty of ammunition, but no handbooks on how to load them. There were books on archery. I took down a crossbow, some arrows and a book with hand-drawn illustrations. The crossbow appealed to my longing for romance and adventure, and it didn't even matter if it was legal or illegal to hunt with them. We had no laws.

I lost a lot of arrows and shattered some, too, as I taught myself to shoot. Working on my aim was next, and I practiced every day.

When I wasn't off in the woods practicing, I weeded my garden. The sun, ever an aphrodisiac, lured me into nudity. It happened so casually, I never dreamed it would become my only lasting contribution to the new social order.

When, in the past, the heat of summer peeled the shirts off workingmen's backs, I'd been jealous of their freedom, denied to women. Bare breasts could be publicly viewed only in the context of entertainment or titillation — or discreet maternity. Road crews, yardmen, construction workers could all get away with stripping to the waist to work, but we'd have been arrested.

None of this was on my mind the first time I stripped. It was not a political statement, it just felt so good, the sun like warm, skilled hands, any breeze like the playful breath of a lover or like shy fingers that want so badly to touch but do not wish to offend, trickling perspiration like a teasing finger. It was more comfortable, yes, without damp cloth sticking to my skin, and it was liberating, too, forbidden before, permissible now. There was an eroticism in undressing I hadn't felt since before BJ left.

Some of the women saw me, and when I did not acknowledge my nudity as unusual, they didn't either. Soon, others began to strip also, when working outdoors. Backs and breasts and arms and bellies grew tanned and looked strong and healthy.

Since no one ever objected, it became a matter of course to see semi-clad women going about a hot day's work.

One of those hot days followed the first nippy night, reminding me of my original plan to knock a hole in the brick wall for a stovepipe.

I'd studied several examples in other houses and it didn't seem that complicated. So I borrowed the pipe from a house that didn't need it anymore.

It was laid out on the lawn and, bare-chested in the sun, I was working up on a ladder, pounding with a borrowed sledgehammer against the brick, when a deep voice said, "Hey, fella, you're not going to get enough draw that way."

Turning to face my critic, I was as surprised by him as he was by me, only I was looking at a bearded face and he was looking at my chest. Both of our mouths fell open.

"Sorry, I thought you were a man," he said.

"Well," I said as I climbed down and walked toward him, "I've been called worse."

With my new awareness of the power of attitude, I refused a remnant of an urge to cover myself.

The stranger was astride a bicycle. (Now why hadn't we thought of that? I wondered.) It was loaded with a bedroll, saddle bags and baskets stuffed with canvas bags. There was a backpack on his back. His beard was reddish, a completely different color from the long blond hair that receded from his forehead.

His blue eyes twinkled as he looked me over. A smile twitched at one corner of his mouth. I stuck out my hand and introduced myself. He looked confused for a second, then shook my hand.

"My name is Steve," he said, "and I don't mean to tell you your business, er, ma'am, but if that pipe is for a woodburner, you've got to extend it above the highest peak of the roof or it won't draw properly."

From his handshake, firm and brief, I sensed his honesty. And the instincts I'd come to rely on told me he was no threat to me.

Then he smiled and I saw his front teeth were slightly separated, and that clinched it. I have always trusted gap-toothed people.

"Oh yeah, Mr. Know-it-all, are you going to sit

there on that bike and criticize, or are you going to lend me a hand?"

He threw back his head and laughed, then set his bicycle on the ground and helped me put up a long stovepipe that we secured to the second-story fascia with wire threaded through eye screws.

Steve unloaded his bike for the trips to the hardware store for the items we needed. His presence in town was of great interest to the others, who soon took up posts on the yard to watch us, or rather, watch *him* work.

There were a hundred questions for him and he answered them all cheerfully as he worked.

He'd come into town from the opposite direction of Nancy and the city. He told of the few people he'd seen, all of them women. He'd stayed two years with an old woman at an all-but-derelict chicken ranch. She thought he was crazy with his talk of a city that perished.

Early in the spring, she'd died in her sleep, never imagining that her handyman was a rarity indeed.

The occasion of a new man in town called for another party, but it was late in the day before anyone thought of it. The next day would have to do.

The women drifted off, but not without shaking his hand or even hugging him. BJ had stayed beside Sandy all afternoon and did not look back at me as they left.

Bereft, I turned to Steve who was gathering up his belongings.

"Look, fella, I don't mean to tell you your

business, but it's kind of late to go house-hunting. Why don't you stay with me for now?"

Which is how I, improbably, came to live with and love a man.

Well, not in any romantic or sexual way. Although I did toy with the notion when trying to think of some way to bug the shit out of BJ.

But even the sweet smell of success couldn't bring me to such a drastic step. Besides, I couldn't work up any sexual feelings for Steve.

In this, I think I was alone in town.

Watching the women vie for his attention was as close to theater as I'd seen so far.

Steve was an easygoing, considerate roommate and, except for the constant flow of gift-bearing women, I had no complaints.

Some friendships are cultivated over time and some are instantaneous. Ours was the latter. We called each other "fella" and laughed together over some of the ploys used on him.

Betty showed up at the door with earrings and makeup on. Carol brought a pair of dead rabbits and hung on every word he said, laughing too loudly and too shrilly at his teasing jests.

Sandy tried to show him what a great dad he would be. BJ tried to convince him to let her manage his career as she saw it.

Maureen and I taunted him when, inevitably, the attention started to go to his head. Invariably, he ended up laughing with us, acknowledging his susceptibility. They were comfortable together, my two friends.

Although she was easily twice his age — he and I were both twenty-five then — she did not mother him, hover over him or cater to him. He loved to tease her about her height, or lack of it.

One day she said something like, "Well, I used to be tall," and he never let her forget it.

It was Steve who thought of fish, of how there might be some in the pond. He had a theory about the "virus," as he called it, having affected only warm-blooded creatures. Maureen challenged his theory, asking where all the frogs and snakes were if that was so.

But she accompanied him to the dam on his fishing expeditions. Always there were fish. They looked fine and tasted wonderful. The women would follow him around, even out there, until he shooed them away. Not Maureen, though. They were inseparable.

One day, long before they realized it, I recognized the faces of people in love.

I said nothing, but observed carefully. I wondered how long it would take them to realize what I already knew.

They were cleaning fish one day, chatting and joking, pretending to flick fish guts and scales at each other. I watched them from inside, watched them having fun. I could hear their voices and I suddenly felt maternal, seeing my friends fall in love.

As Steve pretended to blow fairy dust/fish scales, some must have really been on his hand, because she jumped, and her hand flew to her face.

He quit laughing, got serious and apologetic, and started picking scales from her face. Then he stopped and looked deeply into her eyes. He kissed her. It was their first kiss, I was sure, by the startled look on her face.

As he pulled away she sat there looking stunned.

It was just that one kiss. I was glad I'd seen it. It made me happy inside, gratified, to see them discover the possibilities between them.

Within a week, they were sleeping together, and within a month, she'd moved in with us, sharing his bedroom.

At first she was uncomfortable with me. She said, "I didn't expect to love again, or to be loved, not at my age. And he's so much . . ."

"Smarter? He's so much smarter than you?" I teased.

"Vic! No, not smarter . . ."

"Taller, he is a lot taller even than you used to be."

"No, not taller . . ."

"Nicer? More capable? More valuable?"

"You are not going to make this any easier are you?"

"Maureen, are you just using him?'

"For what? You know better than that!" She was angry now, instantly angry.

"Well then, is he just using you? Is anyone in pain around here? Is anyone crying? Except the village idiots, I mean. Maureen, neither one of you are children. Neither one of you is being manipulated. Neither one of you is mentally deficient. I think you should just give up this age shit. None of that matters now. Just enjoy what you have together, okay? God knows I don't see a lot of happy goings on around here."

"Great advice coming from someone who is eating her heart out over someone who lives just three blocks away."

"Look, that's different. You and Steve have a future. BJ and I have a past. Period."

"Sure. It's all in the past. Sure. That's why you practically dislocate your eyeballs for a glimpse of her. And that's why she always asks about you, how you are, are you happy ..."

"She asks about me? Well, hell, there are only a dozen people living here. She probably asks about all her subjects."

"Would you stop that! She asks, 'How is my girl?' She asked me if I thought there was any way she could get you back!"

"You talked with her about me? Traitor!"

"No, I did not talk with her about you. She asked me and I told her she would have to talk to you about that, about how to get you back."

"You mean in the back? How to get me in the back?"

"Or the sack."

"Maureen!"

"What? Did you think I was too ... old ... for ribald remarks?"

"No, love, I thought you were too tall."

CHAPTER 23

Maureen had given me something to think about.
After all, I had a legitimate excuse — that thin
stack of index cards that was our meager census.

And I was lonely. And I still loved her. I have
never minded, and usually preferred, making the
first move, but only when absolutely certain that the
first move would be welcomed. I told myself I just
needed a little more time.

Steve gave me two new things to think about
while I decided what to do and how to do it.

Autumn was coming fast.

One morning, as we three sat at a breakfast of tomatoes and fish, Steve got a funny look on his face, stood up, walked out the door, climbed on his bike and pedaled madly away.

He hadn't answered any of our questions — What's wrong? What's the matter? Are you all right? He just walked out.

We didn't know what to think, what to make of his odd behavior. I told Maureen that I was sure he'd be back, that he'd explain when he did, not to worry. But I only half meant it. Too many strange things had happened to all of us for me to be sure of anything.

The sun was straight above us when he came home. His bicycle baskets were loaded with what turned out to be cans of peanut butter, canned pork, pork and beans, and plastic jars of honey.

It was like Christmas as he unloaded and explained at the same time.

"When I was on my way here, not that I knew I was coming 'here' here, but I knew there was a town along this route and I pretty much knew what was behind me. Anyway, as I was on my way here, I passed a warehouse. Just sitting there by the side of the road. There was a name painted on the side of the building, a corrugated steel pole barn, that seemed almost familiar, but not quite. This morning it came to me. My sister used to work for that company. They leased warehouse space to the government for surplus food storage — you know, those government giveaways of commodities for the disadvantaged? Well, this morning, as we ate breakfast, it dawned on me what might be in that warehouse. I didn't want to say anything in case I was wrong. I'm sorry, darling" — this to Maureen with a kiss for the top of her head. "But listen, this place has more, lots more food. Some I couldn't carry on the bike. Fifty-pound bags of beans, rice, sugar, flour, salt. Name it. It's ours for the loading."

I knew the right person for the job. "Let's get over to BJ's. She'll know what to do," I said, ignoring the grin on Maureen's face that she tried, for friendship's sake, to stifle.

If BJ was glad to see me, she didn't show it. She listened to what Steve had to say and it was only the fact that I knew her so well that I recognized the gleam in her eye that meant, "I think I can get some mileage out of this."

Within an hour she had the others organized and loaded into the back of a pickup truck that still ran.

She drove, of course. Steve and I sat with her in the cab. It was a close fit, and although we didn't look directly at each other, my thigh where hers touched burned intensely with familiar friction.

At the warehouse, she directed the loading, bucket-brigade-style, and soon her fingers clasped mine too often to be coincidental. When she finally looked me straight in the eye, I was primed for response.

"Beej?" was all I had to say. She took me in her arms and buried her head in my shoulder. I clung to her with all the need of too many lonely nights.

The others stood around and watched, applauding briefly at someone's "It's about time."

On the ride back she kept her right hand on my thigh, and I couldn't squelch a stupid grin.

Yet for all my happiness, I could still sense the tension between BJ and Steve. It has always amazed me when people I've cared about have not liked each other.

BJ's hostility was understandable. She was the leader of a group of women who were, en masse, suddenly infatuated with a red-bearded stranger.

Steve's attachment to Maureen had not quelled the turmoil instigated by his masculine presence.

After unloading the cases and bundles into the grocery store, the others drifted off. Steve and Maureen walked hand-in-hand toward the apartment I had no intention of seeing that night.

Sandy's living in BJ's house had shown a distinct improvement in the level of cleanliness. It reminded me of Nancy, and BJ mentioned that she'd seen her earlier in the summer.

BJ told me without my asking that she'd sent Sandy and the baby to spend the night at Carol's so we could be alone.

It was a conscious and difficult decision not to question their level of intimacy. I just wanted to enjoy this reunion in her bed. But the pillows smelled like Sandy and it was a one-sided encounter. Only BJ's hands were busy, only her mouth, only her tongue.

Orgasm was easy for hair-trigger me, but my mind was not engaged. My attention was on who might have been doing what to whom last night, perhaps even this morning, right here where we lay.

Damn my mouth. I couldn't stop it. I couldn't keep back the words.

"Stop, Beej, stop for a minute."

"Stop? This was always your favorite," she said, extracting her hand from its bowling-ball grip.

"And what's Sandy's favorite?"

"Oh shit, you're not going to start this, are you? Not now, please, Vic. I've missed you so much. Damn it all. Do you know how many nights I damn near came to you and just climbed in bed with you? Tied and gagged you if I had to, just to be with you again?"

"But instead you just rolled over and put your slut to work?"

"Don't start, Vic. I'm warning you."

"What are you going to do? Bully me into submission? Spank me?"

"No, that's her favorite."

"What! Whose?"

"Sandy's. She likes me to spank her. She feels guilty doing something as sinful as lesbian love, I think. If I punish her she can come in peace."

I should have been shocked, or sickened, by this revelation, but somehow it only fascinated me. "That explains a lot."

"Like what?"

"Like the night of my alleged rape attempt. I pulled her hair and she got this funny, spooky look on her face."

"Yeah," BJ said, "Yanking her hair — that's her G-spot. Shuts her up and sends her prone. Every time."

"And what does she do to you," I asked, not really wanting to know, and at the same time needing to know.

BJ lay flat on her back, staring at the ceiling.

Finally she answered. "Nothing. She never touches me. She lets me do her, but she won't even suck my tits."

I knew a cue when I heard one and went to work on BJ so she'd never forget who belonged in her bed.

We slept entwined, Sandy forgotten completely.

In the morning I went home munching a sugar pear from BJ's backyard tree and trying to remember the words of old lust songs.

Steve and Maureen were up, and they shot each other meaningful glances when they thought I wasn't looking.

More trips were planned to the warehouse. BJ didn't expect the truck to hold out much longer and wanted to get in as much of the transport as possible. The warehouse was only nine miles out, but that would seem like a lot when we were walking it and dragging back cases of peanut butter.

We all worked, taking turns on the truck crew or staying at the store to organize the booty.

At the end of the day, each person was rationed six of each item. Since we three lived together, it made for crowded shelf space. It was Steve's idea to use the refrigerator for storage of things like flour and sugar, things that could conceivably be attractive to mice or ants, neither of which we'd seen yet, but still . . .

The refrigerator was one of those kind with separate doors for the refrigerator and freezer compartments.

I'd never opened that refrigerator — afraid, maybe of what sights and smells might await me. Steve had no such qualms. But when he opened it, it was not only totally bare, but turned off. Had Anne been planning an extended stay away?

I opened the freezer. There was something in there, wrapped in aluminum foil, but solid and not smelly. Peeling away the foil, I found Anne's journals. Eleven of them, dating far back into her life and ending the day she left. I held them to me, hugging them like a friend. I slid to the floor and cried.

Eventually, I pulled myself together. Maureen had asked Steve to go for a walk with her. She must have sensed my need to be alone.

I took the journals to my room. Some of them were fancy cloth-covered books, some businesslike black with red corners and binding; some were big, some small, some thick, some thin. One was a lavender legal pad.

I stretched out on my bed, her bed, in the same position she would describe as being the one she used to write in.

In that uncanny way that you can open any book at random, when the wind and stars and moon are right, and happen on a sentence that seems specially written for you, the first sentence I read was: *Is the only pure love an unrealized one?*

At first I skipped around, sampling an insight here, a poem there, a character sketch, a question.

In one segment, she told of reading a great-aunt's journal and being enchanted by the description of a pair of boots this aunt had used two entire weeks' pay to own — $24 in 1918! Then Anne told of doing something similar, only her purple suede boots cost $160. I'd seen those boots; they were still in her closet, much worn.

I read of her grandmother who always, always acted the proper lady among others but wore a red satin slip beneath her widow's black.

I read of her cat Agatha, with an extra claw on each front leg that she used as a thumb for grasping, and who stretched sinuously beside her like a languid lover.

I read a tirade against a woman she'd observed stuffing candies into a crying child's mouth when all the child wanted was to be held.

I learned what she loved and hated and desired and feared. By reading her journals, I felt I knew her better than her talented friends who loved her, better than her parents who could not comprehend her desire to live alone. She was not merely willing to or resigned to living close to the bone. She desired to.

In one passage she spoke of her anguish over *belonging to no world and how do I create one of my own?*

She believed she was bisexual, and she hated the wishy-washiness of it. *How I long to be one or the other, either. Not straight but not truly gay either, does this make me merely cheerful? Strange that I am not happy about it.*

I learned the history of the paintings on her walls. Each was catalogued with an account of its acquisition.

The tobacco leaves in watercolor was a birthday present from a friend, a woman who also painted the tin-roofed farmhouse where they'd planned, someday, to live together. The small abstract in blue and pink and purple had been done by Anne herself. In a combustion of frustrated energy during a 104 degree fever, she'd smeared her face with acrylic paints and laid it repeatedly on the canvas to create a self-portrait.

Anne wrote of rejecting her parents' materialism while admitting an insistence on quality. She laughed at herself, at how she'd mistaken a friend's comment on a new economy car, thinking she'd said "condom car." They'd laughed together at the possibilities this created for safe driving.

She wrote with regret about this same friend finding Mr. Right just as she finally had the courage to admit to her, after ten years of flirting friendship, that she loved her as more than a friend, that she'd harbored secret hopes. The friend had admitted her own feelings for Anne, strong but not strong enough to give up the desire for children, for family, before it was too late.

She wrote of a sexual fantasy she'd had about fried chicken when she tried to become a vegetarian.

One journal was written in two hands. She and another friend sent diaries back and forth instead of letters. The friend mostly recounted the news of that day or what she had for lunch, but sometimes she would break free long enough to tell Anne about her skill at masturbating with the whirlpool jets in her swimming pool as her husband napped on the sofa.

Exhausted, I slept with the journals spread out on the bed with me. Long after dark, BJ did what she said she would do and crept into my bed, scattering the books.

She held me through the night, curled front to my back. In the morning I awoke aroused, and she obliged.

After breakfast, BJ decided to go out to see Nancy and invited me along. It had been quite a while since she'd seen her.

I was actually torn for a moment or two. I'd decided to put Anne's journals into chronological order and read them in one sitting, like a binge.

But I'd been thinking about Nancy, missing her and wondering how she was. So I told BJ I'd go, too. We left early. Steve and Maureen weren't up yet.

On the drive out we sat close, hands on each other's thighs, teasing and tormenting each other and laughing. We hadn't laughed in a long time.

BJ almost overshot the driveway, we were so involved in the flirtation. When she stopped the truck, she turned to me and kissed me deeply, one of those kisses that makes the hair on your toes curl.

Then she pulled back from me and looked at each feature of my face, one at a time with an odd smile on her face.

"I love you, Vic. I'm sorry I'm such a shit sometimes. I hate it when we're apart," she said.

"I don't know. It's almost worth it when we come back together. This has been a great two days, Beej."

"Let's get married," she said with a grin.

"Let's do what?"

"Marry each other, you know, like, 'til death do us part'? Let's get married."

"You really amaze me, Beej, here we are, finally speaking after weeks, months of stubborn silence. And the first thing you say, practically, is let's get married? Is this logical?"

"Well, I don't think marriage ever was much about logic, was it?"

"I think so, yeah, maybe. You know, creating a safe, balanced environment in which to nurture offspring. Economic stability. Assuring goodwill between nations, stuff like that. But I don't see the point, now, for us."

BJ cleaned her fingernails with the corner of her shirt. Finally she spoke.

"I just want there to be something more between us. Something to keep us together. Some pact or agreement to always give us another try before we give us up. I don't want to lose you, Vic, ever."

"You know, you're beautiful when you're sincere."

"Is that yes?"

"No, that's . . . not yet."

"Then it's no."

"No, it's not no either." "Look, as I recall, marriage provided no guarantees. People just gave up anyway, even with it."

"Yeah, well, I've been thinking about that. The way I see it is that's because, when people got married, they sort of picked up their scripts at the door. They started expecting things from each other that they never had any reason to expect. They expected to turn into their parents, only they had two different sets of parents, so they were expecting two different sets of behavior. And, too, they didn't allow for growth, changes in themselves, much less their partners. But we could write that in, sort of, we could define marriage for ourselves as we go along. Cut our own pattern from the inside out."

"And I thought there were no more surprises in our relationship. Do you know that was damn near poetic? Beej, I don't know what to say."

"Just say yes."

"Have you noticed that you don't swear as much as you used to?"

"Noticed? I've been busting my ass to quit! Vic, I want to be worthy of you, and worthy of my people, too. I've been through a lot of changes, we all have, I know, but, I feel like an entirely different person from the way I used to be. I feel . . . strong . . . and able. Valuable. You know? I want my valuable self and your valuable self to promise each other to, oh, I don't know, value each other. I'm getting silly now. I never dreamed I'd have to work so hard just to get a yes out of you."

"Okay."

"Okay? Okay what?"

"Okay, I'll marry you."

"You will?"

I nodded.

"You will! You will! You will! Hot damn!"

She started laying on the horn, deafening me and bringing a disheveled Nancy out onto the back steps.

CHAPTER 24

"BJ? Vic? Oh my God. Thank God you're here!" she cried.

Instead of running to us, a vision I had imagined, she crumpled to the ground, sobbing.

"Nancy?" BJ beat me to Nancy's side. "Nancy? What is it? What's wrong?"

We knelt beside her, sandwiching her in our arms. Smoothing unsmoothable hair, red, so red. I'd forgotten how red her hair was. And I'd forgotten how she could tighten my heart. I looked at BJ and saw tears in her eyes just as I felt my own stream down my face.

Our Nancy was hurting, so we were hurting.

Finally, exhausted, she stopped crying and closed her eyes. We carried her into the house and took her to her room, covering her like a child.

Little Gig was asleep on what had been my bed. Pillows propped him in. BJ and I went to the kitchen and did what Nancy would have done for us. We made tea, and took it to her on a tray.

Dazed, she sat up, her hair like a neon halo. "My friends, oh God, you're really here, I thought I'd dreamed it . . . again."

She looked like she might break down again so we quickly handed her a cup.

"Drink this. It's magic tea," teased BJ.

"Magic? How did it get magic?" Nancy asked with a heartbreakingly childlike hope on her face.

"I made it for you with my hands," said BJ. "My love makes it magic." She pulled me close to her, slipping one arm around me. "Our love makes it magic."

Nancy lowered her head for a minute, then looked up at us and whispered, "I am so thankful you're here. I missed you so much." BJ looked at me and I read her thoughts. I nodded. We would not ask Nancy to explain her emotional outburst until she was calmer.

Gig squeaked, waking up, and Nancy flew to his side. With her out of the room, BJ hugged me quickly, murmuring, "This feels bad, Vic, real bad."

With her baby in her arms, she was again our Nancy, in control, confident, although that strange welcome haunted us for days.

That's how long it took for us to find out what was wrong with Nancy.

But first we had to share our good news. BJ told her.

"Me and Vic, Vic and I, are going to get married. We're going to marry each other, I guess, 'cause I don't know who we'd get to do it for us. Besides, it belongs to us. It's not something that anyone else can do to us."

As she talked, I watched Nancy's face, reading her reactions.

First she looked confused, then disapproving, then reflective. I could almost feel her replay the scene in the yard, then later upstairs. She looked at me, then at BJ, who was silent, waiting for Nancy's blessing.

"I don't know what to say," said Nancy. "You know, you both know, that all of this is against everything I was ever taught." She looked down at her child, then past us out the window.

For a long time, she was silent. A tear trickled down her face that she did not brush away.

She spoke again. "But then, nothing I was ever taught prepared me for any of the things that have happened to us. What is right? What is wrong? Right is to survive. Wrong is ... I don't know. Sometimes wrong is necessary. Is my baby illegitimate? Am I a harlot? Your kind of love I was taught was wrong, was sinful. But you are not bad people and you want to marry. I didn't marry Rich. I don't know, I just don't know." She sounded so sad, defeated.

BJ tried to jolly her out of it. "Geez, Nan, was that your version of congratulations?"

Nancy looked dazed, trying to track what BJ was

saying. She rocked side to side, automatically comforting an already comfortable Gig.

"You want me to say something. I'm sorry, I'm not ... I need to ... happy for you?" Then Nancy clicked back on. "Lord, yes, I'm happy for you. What are you ... when are you ... well, how?"

"We haven't worked out the details yet, have we, Vic? We only just decided. See, we've wasted a lot of time misunderstanding each other, being apart when we didn't need to be. This way, well, we'll be saying — even when you piss me off I'm coming back to you. See?"

Nancy, grinning at me, crossed her eyes and said, "Sounds like love to me."

I laughed, but couldn't shake that feeling that something was wrong, really wrong, with Nancy.

All that day, and the next, she'd become disoriented, suddenly switching off. She'd stop whatever she was doing or saying and go blank. BJ noticed it too, shooting me looks that said, *What the hell?* but neither of us said anything.

Gig had grown, but Nancy still held him ninety percent of his waking hours. BJ and I followed her around, ready to catch her, or him, if she collapsed. She gave us that impression, that she could just crumple into a heap at any second.

She showed us the chickens and goats, and the garden, which was not well tended.

Even when she was Nancy, there was something missing, some undefinable spark. She scolded BJ only once for foul language, but her heart wasn't in it.

BJ and I slept in her old bed. We made love, but quickly and efficiently, as if we were already married. We were both concentrating on the soft crying sounds that came from Nancy's room.

I moved once to go to her, but BJ held me back, saying, "Not yet, she's not ready yet. We have to wait for her. This is Nancy's call."

We danced around each other the next day, too, waiting for some break in Nancy's atmosphere.

It came late the second day. Nancy had not said a word or looked at either of us for a long time. She'd washed Gig with a bucket of water she'd drawn early that morning and allowed to warm in the sun. After his bath, she put the day's diapers in the bucket to soak overnight. Each morning she washed that day's soiled ones and hung them in the sun.

At night, she nursed him to sleep with a blanket covering her breast. It seemed like a quirkily modest gesture, considering. She carried him, all limp and sleeping, to his bed. After Sandy's misfaced baby, I could finally appreciate his flushed-cheek prettiness, damp hair curling over his forehead, lips shiny from Nancy's milk.

When she came downstairs again, she kept her eyes downcast. Immobile, she stood in the middle of the kitchen for what seemed like hours.

BJ was sitting on the other side of the table and I could sense that she, like me, was holding her breath.

Nancy started with the top button of her shirt, slowly unbuttoning it, taking it off. Then the T-shirt she wore underneath, then the skirt and underpants. She stood before us, her face streaming tears as she held her arms out to her sides and turned slowly around.

I heard BJ gasp, or maybe it was me.

Our lovely, kind, decent Nancy was covered with bruises and bite marks. In many places the teeth had broken the skin. There were rope burns at her ankles and wrists, and scars covered the initials carved in her back. RJ.

"Jesus God. Oh, sweet Jesus," said BJ as she rose and went toward Nancy. I rose too, but ran out the kitchen door to vomit in the grass. When I came back in, BJ had wrapped Nancy in the blanket she'd used before to hide from us.

BJ pulled her into her lap and rocked her the way Nancy had rocked Gig. I sat on the floor beside them and held Nancy's hand.

"It was Rich. The last time he came back, he finally noticed Gig. When he saw, you know, how he looks, he went sort of crazy. He stayed here, but he kept saying horrible things about the baby. He said he was going to do things to him. Terrible things. But he didn't. He was different. Mean and . . . sick. He wanted to do sick things to me. He wanted me to . . . to . . . do things to the baby. He wanted to . . . watch. But I wouldn't. I didn't. I never did."

Nancy would break down during her telling; it took a long time to get the whole story.

"He wouldn't help me in the garden or the house or with the baby. He talked to himself, muttering stuff about how he was a man, the only man. He could do anything he wanted. He had rights. Anytime he felt like it he'd force me to . . . Only I don't think it was like he really felt like it either. He just wanted to make me do it. I didn't know what to do. I kept thinking you'd be back soon. Every day I prayed you'd come back. I told him that, finally. I told him when you got here you'd make him stop. Then he started staring at Gig. Staring, just staring. He said, 'That's not mine. That thing is not mine. That is not even human. That is not even animal.' "

BJ took her hand.

"Some days were worse than others. The best days he would just sit in a chair all day not saying anything. The worst days, the worst days he would scream at the baby for crying or for no reason at all. He said he was going to kill him. Said he would put a pillow over him to shut him up. He screamed at the baby to shut up even when he was sleeping. He said he was going to eat him. Cook him and eat him. He tied me up, to the bed. He said he was going to eat me first, then he was going to eat the baby. He bit me, all over. He'd bite and bite, then ... you know ... then bite more. He even knew I was pregnant but he did this to me."

As she sobbed some more, BJ and I looked at each other. In that look was our total agreement.

BJ spoke our verdict. "I'll kill him."

Nancy sobbed harder then, trying to say something at the same time.

BJ tried to calm her, but Nancy fought against comfort. She tore herself away and stood up again. Throwing down the blanket, she raised clenched fists to the ceiling and screamed, "No. No. No. You can't kill him. I already did!"

In stunned silence we heard the rest of her story. When he tired of torturing her, he'd untied her and sent her to cook him something to eat. He fell asleep and Nancy'd gone upstairs with a cast iron skillet. The one she needed two hands to lift.

"I didn't count how many times I hit him. I just kept going until I couldn't lift it anymore. Then I had to rest. Then I pulled him downstairs on the sheet. It took a long time. I had to rest a lot, so it took me a long time."

Nancy stopped. She was no longer crying. BJ covered her again, steering her into the rocker.

A while later, BJ asked, "Nancy? Nancy, where did you put him? Where's Rich?"

Nancy looked at BJ, tried to focus on her face. "Didn't I tell you? I couldn't dig a hole, I was too tired. And I hurt. I was too tired. I put him down the outhouse. I put in a lot of lime, Vic, just like you taught me."

So for two days we'd all pissed on Rich. The warped irony made me laugh. Nancy looked at me and frowned.

"It's not funny, Vic. I killed someone. I took a life. Now I have to die too, and you and BJ have to take care of Gig, okay?"

Terror crossed BJ's face and clenched my heart at the same time.

"No, Nancy," BJ said in a firm voice and slowly, so she'd hear, so she'd comprehend. "No. You were protecting yourself. You had to do it."

But Nancy shook her head. "A life for a life," she said. "That's the law."

"No, Nancy, that's not the law. I am the mayor now. I decide. I say you killed him in self-defense."

For once I was glad BJ was turning authoritarian. I was damned glad for her arrogance at that moment.

I said, "BJ's right, Nancy. Nancy, listen. Did you say you're pregnant? Nancy, did you say that?"

She nodded.

"So, you see, you were also protecting your baby. And Gig. Nancy, he would have killed Gig, you know he would have. Nancy, think about Gig."

Nancy focused again, at me then at BJ. Her son's name was the magic word.

She gathered up her clothes and went naked to her room, shutting the door behind her.

In the morning, we decided to move them into town, along with as many chickens as we could catch and put in the back of the truck. We tied the goats to the rear bumper with rope.

We urinated in the weeds. I refused to look in the outhouse, and I never asked BJ if she did.

There was only one thing I wanted from the house besides Nancy. Anne's journals had inspired me. In the attic I found the blank book, *Moments Together*. The title seemed very appropriate.

We drove slowly home.

CHAPTER 25

We moved them into the apartment next door to mine. We told only Maureen and Steve the whole story. Maureen cried and gingerly placed her arms around Nancy. Nancy patted her, comforting the comforter.

Nancy hardly spoke for two years, and then only to us. She would not look anyone in the eye. Maureen delivered her babies. Triplets, for God's sake, as if Rich's spiteful sperm knew their time was up and hurried to do as much damage as they could.

The women were wonderful to Nancy. Everyone helped with all the babies. Eventually, it would have been difficult to say which children were whose. Everyone cares for everyone else's as if they were their own. There were more babies, too.

Maureen urged Steve to service those who wished it. He was dubious at first and never has really enjoyed the job. He absolutely adores Maureen, and told me once that he closes his eyes and pretends he is with her whenever he has a "job to do," as he says.

Once the women understood that they could have him, but never *have* him, they didn't bother him much. In fact, eventually, they came to approach Maureen to set up meetings with Steve. There is no sneaking around, no secrets, no cheating, no lies, no deceit, and no problems.

Except for Sandy, of course, who would periodically try to get more from Steve than sex. He never spends the night anywhere but with Maureen, and he never eats the food Sandy will still sometimes prepare for him, but brings it home to share with Maureen.

Things have changed little. The lights haven't come on suddenly. We did not wake up to find it all a horrible dream. We have all survived by doing whatever we have to do, but there has been time for laughter, and love.

BJ and I never did get married, not in any ceremonial sense. We've never even mentioned it. Ghosts, I guess, bad memories.

We continue to live apart, but visit frequently. We've learned to talk over misunderstandings. We even fight, not often but constructively. We love each other in quieter, deeper ways now, though lovemaking has never become routine.

Mostly we just make love with each other, but sometimes one or the other will be with someone else. Her and Sandy. Me and Carol. But we always discuss it first, if possible, or as soon afterwards as we can. Sex now has less to do with passion than with comfort and closeness.

Carol and I just happened. She came to visit me one day and told me how she ached for human touch. She felt as if she were mica, leaving flakes of herself wherever she went, as if she were disintegrating and would soon cease to exist.

I'd come to care for her, so I began to massage her neck and shoulders, her back. Through her tears, she whispered, "Touch me." So I did. When I told BJ, she understood.

I've never learned to like Sandy or to trust her, but since BJ likes her, I tolerate her.

Steve and Maureen moved down to the apartment on the other side of Nancy. Goats and chickens wander the yards freely. Betty is pregnant now. Steve is working on a plan to open up the walls between apartments and build walk-through fireplaces, but it seems too ambitious a project for me. However.

I have a new friend now, living with me. She came out of the woods and claimed me. She is black and huge and sleek. A cat to care for me. She seems perfectly normal to look at until you notice her eyes, double pupiled and hypnotic. I guessed her name was Martha, and when I asked her, she blinked slowly. So I continue to call her Martha. I fantasize sometimes that my Martha comes here and finds me, but then her face becomes BJ's. Sometimes I imagine Anne coming home too, but realistically I know that if she meant to come home, she'd probably be here by now.

Mostly we all live in peace. We're too busy surviving to fight. The babies are all deformed, in different ways. No two alike. On the outside at least. When Gig and little Jane were playing one day, I noticed for the first time the nature of their similarity. Gig learned to walk, sort of, penguin-like, but could not grasp things very far out of his reach.

I watched little Jane hand him things he wanted without being asked. It occurred to me to watch the children more closely. Until then, I have to admit, I'd pretty much ignored them.

They always played in harmony, none of the childhood squabbles I'd been taught were normal. The triplets, too, played cooperatively. I watched for two more years, trying to comprehend something that defied my studies in education.

Finally I saw it. The hairs on my arms stood up with the realization. These children were our opposites. We all looked pretty much alike on the outside, but inside we were all different. These new people were all different on the outside, often grotesquely so — even the triplets which had shared Nancy's womb and a common gene pool were completely different-looking from one another.

But inside, in their hearts and minds, they were identical. Like-souled, perhaps, they had a common spirit.

If one is sick or hurt, they all cry. If one is tickled, they all laugh. They talk, some with difficulty, but they seldom do, at least with each other. I suspect telepathy or something similar but more elemental.

They fascinate me now. I waited a long time to start *Moments Together,* until Nancy came out of her self-imposed near-silence. She broke it by reading to her babies. I came across her in the yard as she sat under a tree, reading to them from her Bible. I lay down under the tree and put my head in her lap, tears in my eyes. She stroked my hair as if I were just one of the children, come to her for affection, and kept reading.

I began the journal as a kind of history, a written record of what brought us here. But I soon realized what a relief it was to be able to tell my secrets to these pages. I've tried to not make anyone seem worse or better than they are, but love and hate still exist in my generation.

One night I dreamed that the children were all grown, only in my dream there were dozens of them. They circled around Nancy, BJ and me as we stood with our backs together. The children were laughing, teasing us about how funny we looked, with two eyes, one nose, one mouth and three of nothing. They circled around us as in a dance but spiraled outward to cover the earth.

I woke from this dream in tears. Remnants of old pain were fresh in my mouth like the copper taste of blood.

Our children, in reality, do not have it in them to taunt, to torment. There is a gentleness in them that is frightening. Exercising obsolete thought patterns, I wonder sometimes, how will they survive? How will they protect themselves?

Then I laugh at myself. Protect themselves from what?

We have always been our own worst enemies, but that has been bred out of these new ones.

Maureen has asked me several times why don't I try for a child of my own. She's seen me fall in love with these others. But they are mine, too, and all I need. I have never had a man inside me, and even though Steve is a good friend, well my heart just isn't in it.

What I do now is write, in longhand. My handwriting changes with the intensity of my memories, and now I am writing in tiny print, the pages almost used up. I am almost finished with this book. The next one will be observations of the children. How they grow, how they learn; if they have children, will theirs be throwbacks — full of hates and fears and jealousies and ambitions, like us, or will they continue this evolution, externally unique and internally identical? Will there be separations between them? Will they decide who is acceptable to love and who is not? Or will they love us as we are learning to do, based on each person's capacity to love?

The other thing I do, have in fact just started to do, again, is teach. This time it's different. I am going to teach them whatever I can, in exchange and in gratitude for all they are teaching me.

A few of the publications of
THE NAIAD PRESS, INC.
P.O. Box 10543 • Tallahassee, Florida 32302
Phone (904) 539-5965
Mail orders welcome. Please include 15% postage.

SAVING GRACE by Jennifer Fulton. 224 pp. Adventure and romantic entanglement. ISBN 1-56280-051-5 $9.95

THE YEAR SEVEN by Molleen Zanger. 208 pp. Women surviving in a new world. ISBN 1-56280-034-5   9.95

CURIOUS WINE by Katherine V. Forrest. 176 pp. Tenth Anniversary Edition. The most popular contemporary Lesbian love story. ISBN 1-56280-053-1   9.95

CHAUTAUQUA by Catherine Ennis. 192 pp. Exciting, romantic adventure. ISBN 1-56280-032-9   9.95

A PROPER BURIAL by Pat Welch. 192 pp. Third in the Helen Black mystery series. ISBN 1-56280-033-7   9.95

SILVERLAKE HEAT: A Novel of Suspense by Carol Schmidt. 240 pp. Rhonda is as hot as Laney's dreams. ISBN 1-56280-031-0   9.95

LOVE, ZENA BETH by Diane Salvatore. 224 pp. The most talked about lesbian novel of the nineties! ISBN 1-56280-030-2   9.95

A DOORYARD FULL OF FLOWERS by Isabel Miller. 160 pp. Stories incl. 2 sequels to *Patience and Sarah.* ISBN 1-56280-029-9   9.95

MURDER BY TRADITION by Katherine V. Forrest. 288 pp. A Kate Delafield Mystery. 4th in a series. ISBN 1-56280-002-7   9.95

THE EROTIC NAIAD edited by Katherine V. Forrest & Barbara Grier. 224 pp. Love stories by Naiad Press authors. ISBN 1-56280-026-4   12.95

DEAD CERTAIN by Claire McNab. 224 pp. 5th Det. Insp. Carol Ashton mystery. ISBN 1-56280-027-2   9.95

CRAZY FOR LOVING by Jaye Maiman. 320 pp. 2nd Robin Miller mystery. ISBN 1-56280-025-6   9.95

STONEHURST by Barbara Johnson. 176 pp. Passionate regency romance. ISBN 1-56280-024-8   9.95

INTRODUCING AMANDA VALENTINE by Rose Beecham. 256 pp. An Amanda Valentine Mystery — 1st in a series. ISBN 1-56280-021-3   9.95

UNCERTAIN COMPANIONS by Robbi Sommers. 204 pp. Steamy, erotic novel. ISBN 1-56280-017-5   9.95

A TIGER'S HEART by Lauren W. Douglas. 240 pp. Fourth Caitlin
Reece Mystery.   ISBN 1-56280-018-3   9.95

PAPERBACK ROMANCE by Karin Kallmaker. 256 pp. A
delicious romance.   ISBN 1-56280-019-1   9.95

MORTON RIVER VALLEY by Lee Lynch. 304 pp. Lee Lynch at
her best!   ISBN 1-56280-016-7   9.95

THE LAVENDER HOUSE MURDER by Nikki Baker. 224 pp. A
Virginia Kelly Mystery. Second in a series.   ISBN 1-56280-012-4   9.95

PASSION BAY by Jennifer Fulton. 224 pp. Passionate romance,
virgin beaches, tropical skies.   ISBN 1-56280-028-0   9.95

STICKS AND STONES by Jackie Calhoun. 208 pp. Contemporary
lesbian lives and loves.   ISBN 1-56280-020-5   9.95

DELIA IRONFOOT by Jeane Harris. 192 pp. Adventure for Delia
and Beth in the Utah mountains.   ISBN 1-56280-014-0   9.95

UNDER THE SOUTHERN CROSS by Claire McNab. 192 pp.
Romantic nights Down Under.   ISBN 1-56280-011-6   9.95

RIVERFINGER WOMEN by Elana Nachman/Dykewomon.
208 pp. Classic Lesbian/feminist novel.   ISBN 1-56280-013-2   8.95

A CERTAIN DISCONTENT by Cleve Boutell. 240 pp. A unique
coterie of women.   ISBN 1-56280-009-4   9.95

GRASSY FLATS by Penny Hayes. 256 pp. Lesbian romance in
the '30s.   ISBN 1-56280-010-8   9.95

A SINGULAR SPY by Amanda K. Williams. 192 pp. 3rd spy novel
featuring Lesbian agent Madison McGuire.   ISBN 1-56280-008-6   8.95

THE END OF APRIL by Penny Sumner. 240 pp. A Victoria Cross
Mystery. First in a series.   ISBN 1-56280-007-8   8.95

A FLIGHT OF ANGELS by Sarah Aldridge. 240 pp. Romance set at
the National Gallery of Art   ISBN 1-56280-001-9   9.95

HOUSTON TOWN by Deborah Powell. 208 pp. A Hollis Carpenter
mystery. Second in a series.   ISBN 1-56280-006-X   8.95

KISS AND TELL by Robbi Sommers. 192 pp. Scorching stories by
the author of *Pleasures*.   ISBN 1-56280-005-1   9.95

STILL WATERS by Pat Welch. 208 pp. Second in the Helen
Black mystery series.   ISBN 0-941483-97-5   9.95

MURDER IS GERMANE by Karen Saum. 224 pp. The 2nd
Brigid Donovan mystery.   ISBN 0-941483-98-3   8.95

TO LOVE AGAIN by Evelyn Kennedy. 208 pp. Wildly
romantic love story.   ISBN 0-941483-85-1   9.95

IN THE GAME by Nikki Baker. 192 pp. A Virginia Kelly
mystery. First in a series.   ISBN 01-56280-004-3   9.95

AVALON by Mary Jane Jones. 256 pp. A Lesbian Arthurian
romance.   ISBN 0-941483-96-7   9.95

STRANDED by Camarin Grae. 320 pp. Entertaining, riveting
adventure.   ISBN 0-941483-99-1   9.95

THE DAUGHTERS OF ARTEMIS by Lauren Wright Douglas.
240 pp. Third Caitlin Reece mystery.   ISBN 0-941483-95-9   9.95

CLEARWATER by Catherine Ennis. 176 pp. Romantic secrets
of a small Louisiana town.   ISBN 0-941483-65-7   8.95

THE HALLELUJAH MURDERS by Dorothy Tell. 176 pp.
Second Poppy Dillworth mystery.   ISBN 0-941483-88-6   8.95

ZETA BASE by Judith Alguire. 208 pp. Lesbian triangle
on a future Earth.   ISBN 0-941483-94-0   9.95

SECOND CHANCE by Jackie Calhoun. 256 pp. Contemporary
Lesbian lives and loves.   ISBN 0-941483-93-2   9.95

BENEDICTION by Diane Salvatore. 272 pp. Striking,
contemporary romantic novel.   ISBN 0-941483-90-8   9.95

CALLING RAIN by Karen Marie Christa Minns. 240 pp.
Spellbinding, erotic love story   ISBN 0-941483-87-8   9.95

BLACK IRIS by Jeane Harris. 192 pp. Caroline's hidden past . . .
                                           ISBN 0-941483-68-1   8.95

TOUCHWOOD by Karin Kallmaker. 240 pp. Loving, May/
December romance.   ISBN 0-941483-76-2   9.95

BAYOU CITY SECRETS by Deborah Powell. 224 pp. A Hollis
Carpenter mystery. First in a series.   ISBN 0-941483-91-6   9.95

COP OUT by Claire McNab. 208 pp. 4th Det. Insp. Carol Ashton
mystery.   ISBN 0-941483-84-3   9.95

LODESTAR by Phyllis Horn. 224 pp. Romantic, fast-moving
adventure.   ISBN 0-941483-83-5   8.95

THE BEVERLY MALIBU by Katherine V. Forrest. 288 pp. A
Kate Delafield Mystery. 3rd in a series.   ISBN 0-941483-48-7   9.95

THAT OLD STUDEBAKER by Lee Lynch. 272 pp. Andy's affair
with Regina and her attachment to her beloved car.
                                           ISBN 0-941483-82-7   9.95

PASSION'S LEGACY by Lori Paige. 224 pp. Sarah is swept into
the arms of Augusta Pym in this delightful historical romance.
                                           ISBN 0-941483-81-9   8.95

THE PROVIDENCE FILE by Amanda Kyle Williams. 256 pp.
Second espionage thriller featuring lesbian agent Madison McGuire
                                           ISBN 0-941483-92-4   8.95

I LEFT MY HEART by Jaye Maiman. 320 pp. A Robin Miller
Mystery. First in a series.   ISBN 0-941483-72-X   9.95

THE PRICE OF SALT by Patricia Highsmith (writing as Claire
Morgan). 288 pp. Classic lesbian novel, first issued in 1952 . . .
acknowledged by its author under her own, very famous, name.
                                           ISBN 1-56280-003-5   9.95

SIDE BY SIDE by Isabel Miller. 256 pp. From beloved author of
Patience and Sarah.   ISBN 0-941483-77-0   9.95

SOUTHBOUND by Sheila Ortiz Taylor. 240 pp. Hilarious sequel
to *Faultline.*   ISBN 0-941483-78-9   8.95

STAYING POWER: LONG TERM LESBIAN COUPLES
by Susan E. Johnson. 352 pp. Joys of coupledom.
                                                      ISBN 0-941-483-75-4   12.95

SLICK by Camarin Grae. 304 pp. Exotic, erotic adventure.
                                                      ISBN 0-941483-74-6   9.95

NINTH LIFE by Lauren Wright Douglas. 256 pp. A Caitlin
Reece mystery. 2nd in a series.   ISBN 0-941483-50-9   8.95

PLAYERS by Robbi Sommers. 192 pp. Sizzling, erotic novel.
                                                      ISBN 0-941483-73-8   9.95

MURDER AT RED ROOK RANCH by Dorothy Tell. 224 pp.
First Poppy Dillworth adventure.   ISBN 0-941483-80-0   8.95

LESBIAN SURVIVAL MANUAL by Rhonda Dicksion.
112 pp. Cartoons!   ISBN 0-941483-71-1   8.95

A ROOM FULL OF WOMEN by Elisabeth Nonas. 256 pp.
Contemporary Lesbian lives.   ISBN 0-941483-69-X   9.95

MURDER IS RELATIVE by Karen Saum. 256 pp. The first
Brigid Donovan mystery.   ISBN 0-941483-70-3   8.95

PRIORITIES by Lynda Lyons 288 pp. Science fiction with
a twist.   ISBN 0-941483-66-5   8.95

THEME FOR DIVERSE INSTRUMENTS by Jane Rule. 208
pp. Powerful romantic lesbian stories.   ISBN 0-941483-63-0   8.95

LESBIAN QUERIES by Hertz & Ertman. 112 pp. The questions
you were too embarrassed to ask.   ISBN 0-941483-67-3   8.95

CLUB 12 by Amanda Kyle Williams. 288 pp. Espionage thriller
featuring a lesbian agent!   ISBN 0-941483-64-9   8.95

DEATH DOWN UNDER by Claire McNab. 240 pp. 3rd Det.
Insp. Carol Ashton mystery.   ISBN 0-941483-39-8   9.95

MONTANA FEATHERS by Penny Hayes. 256 pp. Vivian and
Elizabeth find love in frontier Montana.   ISBN 0-941483-61-4   8.95

CHESAPEAKE PROJECT by Phyllis Horn. 304 pp. Jessie &
Meredith in perilous adventure.   ISBN 0-941483-58-4   8.95

LIFESTYLES by Jackie Calhoun. 224 pp. Contemporary Lesbian
lives and loves.   ISBN 0-941483-57-6   9.95

VIRAGO by Karen Marie Christa Minns. 208 pp. Darsen has
chosen Ginny.   ISBN 0-941483-56-8   8.95

WILDERNESS TREK by Dorothy Tell. 192 pp. Six women on
vacation learning ''new'' skills.   ISBN 0-941483-60-6   8.95

MURDER BY THE BOOK by Pat Welch. 256 pp. A Helen
Black Mystery. First in a series.   ISBN 0-941483-59-2   9.95

BERRIGAN by Vicki P. McConnell. 176 pp. Youthful Lesbian —
romantic, idealistic Berrigan.   ISBN 0-941483-55-X   8.95

LESBIANS IN GERMANY by Lillian Faderman & B. Eriksson.
128 pp. Fiction, poetry, essays.   ISBN 0-941483-62-2   8.95

THERE'S SOMETHING I'VE BEEN MEANING TO TELL
YOU Ed. by Loralee MacPike. 288 pp. Gay men and lesbians
coming out to their children.   ISBN 0-941483-44-4   9.95

LIFTING BELLY by Gertrude Stein. Ed. by Rebecca Mark. 104
pp. Erotic poetry.   ISBN 0-941483-51-7   8.95

ROSE PENSKI by Roz Perry. 192 pp. Adult lovers in a long-term
relationship.   ISBN 0-941483-37-1   8.95

AFTER THE FIRE by Jane Rule. 256 pp. Warm, human novel
by this incomparable author.   ISBN 0-941483-45-2   8.95

SUE SLATE, PRIVATE EYE by Lee Lynch. 176 pp. The gay
folk of Peacock Alley are *all cats.*   ISBN 0-941483-52-5   8.95

CHRIS by Randy Salem. 224 pp. Golden oldie. Handsome Chris
and her adventures.   ISBN 0-941483-42-8   8.95

THREE WOMEN by March Hastings. 232 pp. Golden oldie. A
triangle among wealthy sophisticates.   ISBN 0-941483-43-6   8.95

RICE AND BEANS by Valeria Taylor. 232 pp. Love and
romance on poverty row.   ISBN 0-941483-41-X   8.95

PLEASURES by Robbi Sommers. 204 pp. Unprecedented
eroticism.   ISBN 0-941483-49-5   8.95

EDGEWISE by Camarin Grae. 372 pp. Spellbinding
adventure.   ISBN 0-941483-19-3   9.95

FATAL REUNION by Claire McNab. 224 pp. 2nd Det. Inspec.
Carol Ashton mystery.   ISBN 0-941483-40-1   8.95

KEEP TO ME STRANGER by Sarah Aldridge. 372 pp. Romance
set in a department store dynasty.   ISBN 0-941483-38-X   9.95

HEARTSCAPE by Sue Gambill. 204 pp. American lesbian in
Portugal.   ISBN 0-941483-33-9   8.95

IN THE BLOOD by Lauren Wright Douglas. 252 pp. Lesbian
science fiction adventure fantasy   ISBN 0-941483-22-3   8.95

These are just a few of the many Naiad Press titles — we are the oldest and
largest lesbian/feminist publishing company in the world. Please request a
complete catalog. We offer personal service; we encourage and welcome direct
mail orders from individuals who have limited access to bookstores carrying
our publications.